FOUR HANDS FOR MERCY

FOUR
HANDS
for
MERCY

by **MARY N. DOLIM**
and **GEN KAKACEK**

D. VAN NOSTRAND COMPANY, INC.
Princeton, New Jersey   toronto new york london

D. VAN NOSTRAND COMPANY, INC.
120 Alexander St., Princeton, New Jersey (*Principal office*)
24 West 40 Street, New York 18, New York

D. VAN NOSTRAND COMPANY, LTD.
358, Kensington High Street, London, W.14, England

D. VAN NOSTRAND COMPANY (Canada), LTD.
25 Hollinger Road, Toronto 16, Canada

Published simultaneously in Canada by
D. VAN NOSTRAND COMPANY (Canada), LTD.

Library of Congress Catalog Card No. 65-25532

For Patrushka

Acknowledgments

The authors wish to thank a fine young nurse,

ANN K. MIRANDA

*for technical advice and for reading the book in
manuscript*

and two teachers of nursing,

MURIEL ALFORD & EDITH GASSNER

*who, by their instruction and example, have given
the world many dedicated nurses.*

Contents

1

Heart in Hand

As the first sound of the siren cut through the August afternoon, Julia opened the third-floor dormitory window and leaned out. Stretching, she leaned farther, inches beyond safety, inches short of a satisfactory view. Near, nearer came the wail until, abruptly, the crescendo of sound dropped to a growl as the red ambulance turned in at the Emergency Entrance to Mercy Hospital. She could see two men in white scurrying, but a line of cedars blanked the ambulance's rear door from sight. On the sidewalk directly below, a gray-haired woman flailed her arms in dismay at Julia's dangerous perch.

The door to her room swung open. Then came a gasp, "OHMIGOSH!" and the thud of dropped suitcases.

Julia started and whirled, bumping her head on the window sash and her knee on the radiator. "You frightened me."

"*I frightened you!*" The plump cinnamon-haired girl at the doorway bent to pick up her luggage, slid it into the room and plopped on the nearest twin bed. "Are you a manic depressive or a practicing acrobat?"

Julia rubbed the lump beneath one short blonde wave

and laughed. "If you must have a diagnosis, I guess it would be acute unsatisfied curiosity, complicated by demerits, unless that woman waving me away from the window was just a passing stranger."

"Probably Ma Marsh, the housemother. She was going out as I came in. Oh, I'm Rosemary Dowling from Clearview. One misplaced suitcase, one missed bus, and one taxi's flat tire from here. Did I miss much this morning?"

"Book issue and a welcome speech. We have a hospital orientation tour this afternoon . . . at two o'clock. After that we're free to unpack and get settled. Did I introduce myself? I'm Julia Rogers from San Dorcas."

"San Dorcas? There must be a dozen nursing schools between there and here. How'd you decide to come to San Francisco?"

"Our doctor's office nurse graduated from Mercy. She recommended it and my high school counselor agreed that it's one of the best. A hundred miles isn't far. One of the girls from San Dorcas is going to the University of Pennsylvania. That I call far from home."

"As of now, Mercy is home but this room needs a lot of something. I brought along spreads—charcoal chenille—and some white crisscross curtains. But I like your contribution far better. Who is that dreamy fellow?"

"Paul Hammond," Julia said with quick pride, her blue eyes caressing the gold-framed picture on the desk. "Private Paul Hammond, U. S. Marine Corps."

Rosemary picked up the picture and read aloud, " 'You belong to me! Paul.' Now there's a positive approach. Are you as sure of him as all that?"

"We're engaged, sort of unofficially. But the day I graduate we'll . . . oh, look at the time. We have to be in uniform for the tour so we'd better . . ."

"In uniform by two o'clock! I'll be lucky if I can *find* my uniforms by two o'clock." Her glance followed Julia's to the closet door where a size ten blue-striped underdress and white-bibbed apron hung in gleaming, just-pressed splendor. "Come to think of it, mine's as big as a tent and who could misplace a tent? The color of this room reminds me of a strawberry malt and I don't even remember lunch. Maybe I can find a candy machine."

From far down the hall came a voice calling, "Phone for Dowling. Is there a freshman named Dowling up there?"

Sighing, Rosemary climbed over her luggage, smoothed the lace-edged collar of her pink gingham and sighed again as she stepped into the hall. "Here, I'm Dowling."

"Long distance."

"I know. I know." To Julia she said, "My mother is . . . motherly. She just can't believe I could get from there to here."

"You almost didn't, remember?" Julia teased.

"Roommate, be a roommate." Rosemary said as she left. "Not more, not less."

Be a roommate, Julia mulled. Since I've never been a roommate I don't know how. She knew how to be a sister, a less than satisfactory sister, according to fourteen-year-old John, but she seemed to suit Mike just fine. Seven was an altogether easier age to sister than fourteen. She knew how to be a daughter. Walter and Mary Rogers often showed their pleasure in her in the unspoken language of exchanged glances although they teased about how her slumber parties, her various puppy loves, her freckle creams, and the constantly ringing phone had aged them.

She knew how to be a friend. Her room at home had been giggle headquarters for half a dozen girls and she had held the title of Best Friend to Betsy Matthews since third grade. Only three days ago she had given a bridal shower for Betsy and would be her maid of honor in October. After

3

that Betsy would follow Phil wherever his construction job took him, but their friendship would not end because of separate paths. Yes, she knew how to be a friend. But a roommate? I am totally unqualified owing to lack of experience, Miss Dowling. But roommates are assigned. I am, therefore, a roommate.

What I really don't know how to be is a nurse.

She shed her rolled cuff blouse and plaid cotton skirt, slipped into the shapeless blue underdress and struggled with the shank-buttons of the fitted bib apron. She half expected to hear her mother call, "Nap time, Julie. Time to pack up your Little Nurse Kit." But she was a hundred miles from home and twelve years past the time of candy pills and plastic thermometers. For five hours she'd been a student nurse at Mercy Hospital but she felt less a nurse now than when she'd worn a paper cap and bandaged up old Prince's imaginary wounds.

Could that staggering number of books and her own willingness turn her into a nurse? Does a glass slipper turn a girl into a princess? Julia Rogers, you are going to be a nurse. She wandered to the window and watched the red ambulance glide into the street traffic. If you don't fall on your head and become a patient instead.

Unhurried, amiably smiling, Rosemary strolled back into the room, a tall glass of milk and an eight-high stack of graham crackers balanced on one hand and the last of her luggage clutched in the other. "Someone named Archer just introduced me into that heartwarming nook called the nurses' kitchen. I feel comforted that a freshman is allowed hunger pangs. Say, you look like a regular Nightingale, Julia."

"Thanks, but I feel like an impostor."

Down the hall a radio blared into action, the raucous bleat of a trio racing a twanged guitar. "Ohmigosh," Rose-

4

mary leaped to the door, "The night nurses will be wide awake!" But the noise became, suddenly, silence. Rising whispers of conversation and rubber-soled shoes filled the hallway.

"Night nurses? How'd you know to think of them?"

"My sister graduated from here five years ago. I guess I absorbed more of her talk than I'd realized. I do wish I could remember which suitcase has my uniforms. My mother packed and I don't know. . . ." She flicked the lock on the train case, murmured, "I might have known," and extracted a neatly typed note. "Duty shoes and stockings in the wardrobe case. Uniforms in the Pullman case. Don't forget to rinse out your nylons tonight. Love, Mother." She gulped the last of her milk and said, "You'd think forty miles was too far for apron strings to stretch, wouldn't you?"

Julia, pulling on her white nylons and struggling with her stiff white duty oxfords, wanted to answer but what kind of reply could she give to such a question? With no hope of appearing subtle, she changed the subject. "There's an ironing board in the room at the end of the hall."

A hesitant knock at the open door gave the impression of considerably less poise than the person it announced displayed. Shining brown hair pulled back to a neat chignon, just a touch of makeup to emphasize her elegant high-boned face, her stiff-starched apron giving her an air of having invented the profession, the girl at the door offered, "Since you're pushed for time I'll iron your apron, Rosemary."

Looking at her Julia felt as crumpled as a soggy towel.

"Hello again and aren't you nice! Oh, this is my roommate, Julia Rogers. Julia, this is—"

"Lou Ellen Archer," the girl volunteered. "We met this morning, in a general way. I didn't see you at lunch, Rogers. Did you get lost?"

A flash of crimson in her cheeks made a half truth impossible. Julia conquered the moment and Lou Ellen's grand manner with one syllable. "Yes."

"I would have too except that I've been here to lunch many times. My father and the chief of staff are cronies. Rosemary, do find that apron. We have to be downstairs in fourteen minutes and the spray starch does take a minute or two to apply."

Spray starch, Julia accused the gentle folds of her own apron. Why couldn't you think of that?

Admitting Office . . . a single red rose in a crystal vase and a low-voiced, kindly woman in a silk print, hand poised over the record sheet that reduced symptoms and emotions to name, hospital number, diagnosis, neat little blanks which turned a person into a patient.

Record Room . . . last week's, last year's triumphs of healing, blessed relief from pain, sudden endings or bright beginnings of life recorded and retained on film.

Pharmacy, X-ray . . . where Mrs. Braddock led, thirty-two anxious, interested freshmen followed. Mrs. Braddock, director of nursing education, her dark hair streaked white at the temples and pulled into a tight bun below her white graduate cap, had in her manner something of a teacher and something of a mother. Whispers fluttered through the group. "Conversation later, please, young ladies." She spoke with a soft, assured voice. Julia warmed to her at once and walked close to hear each quiet explanation of hospital routine.

Laboratory . . . body chemistry explored a thousand ways by medical detectives bent on catching the villain virus, the wily coccus. An intelligent question from Lou Ellen Archer was rewarded by an approving nod from the pathologist. "You've had college chemistry," he said, and gave her five minutes of answer which left the rest of the freshmen feeling awkward and not very bright.

Emergency Room . . . Mrs. Braddock paused at the closed door and said, "Wait here a moment." She opened the door and stepped inside just long enough to see two nurses and a doctor bent over a small boy on a narrow bed-like gurney. "We'll come back a bit later when we won't be in the way." Julia caught sight of the little fellow's eyes, blue and large with hurt. She tried to smile at him but Mrs. Braddock closed the door, blanking out the sound of his sobs.

Surgical Floor, Intensive Care Ward, Recovery Room . . . New sights, new sounds, in every area the swish of rubber soles, graduates, students, aids, maids, volunteers, technicians, residents, dieticians . . . a wide variety of uniforms, a wider variety of faces . . . a never-ceasing hum of activity, all for one cause: the patient. Julia could not move her mind or her heart away from the small blue-eyed boy in the Emergency Room.

Then, her thoughts tumbling backward to a long ago day, she knew why the little fellow seemed so familiar. He was the image of Tommy Stinson, the youngster who more than anyone else had led her to this hospital corridor. When she first baby-sat for five-year-old Tommy he had been a pitiful sight—face blue-gray, every breath a gasp. But, months later, the miracle of heart surgery had transformed him into a pink-cheeked rascal of a boy, his blue eyes sparkling with mischief. She had always been inclined toward nursing but once she saw what doctors and nurses did for little Tommy her choice of careers was never in serious doubt. In fact the only doubt had come last Christmas when Paul wanted to get married.

Surgery . . . gleaming tile and stainless steel, a glance into a busy operating room and a long look through an unoc-

7

cupied one. Work room tables piled high with oiled instruments, technicians sorting kellys, hemastats, mosquito clamps for tomorrow's surgery schedule. Linen room bundles marked *Laparotomy, T&A, D&C, Ortho.* Bright-lidded sterilizers, and a round-doored autoclave. Would she ever, ever know and understand all these words, know all these places, come to be a useful part of the hospital team? Would she ever help right a heart which nature had let grow wrong?

Obstetrics . . . Mrs. Braddock stopped the group at the white double doors leading to the O.B. wing. "We'll have to see this area another time." she said. "There are two deliveries underway and a third one imminent. I'm afraid we'd be in the—" A young blond doctor whizzed by, stethoscope dangling from the hip pocket of his white uniform. The doors flip-flopped behind him.

Heedless of the director's warning, Betty Martin dimpled and exclaimed, "That's the most interesting sight I've seen today!"

With a hint of a grin, Mrs. Braddock said, "The doors, Miss Martin? Yes, they are of interest, double-hinged so they open either way and wide enough to allow a hospital bed to be pushed through. If you've examined the doors thoroughly, young ladies, we'll go to Medical Service. Up these stairs and to the left, please."

Medical Floor . . . Signs: Oxygen, No Smoking. Measured Output. No Visitors. Slow dying and quick antibiotic cures. A young man flushed with fever. An old man gray with pain. Lights flashing for attention. A wall speaker calling: "Dr. Langdon, Emergency Room. Dr. Langdon, Emergency. Dr. Langdon, Emergency." Julia's heart leaped. Was Dr. Langdon being summoned for Little Blue Eyes? Was he worse? Was he . . . was he . . . ?

"This is the linen room and this is the utility room," Mrs. Braddock explained. "The medicines are kept by the

8

Nurses' Station and the charts are. . . ." Julia's vision was blurred by tears and her own questions blotted out the director's words. Why were there no tears in Mrs. Braddock's eyes? Didn't she care about that little fellow? How could you be a good nurse if you didn't care?

Pediatric Wing . . . A flannel-gowned miss of two, bouncing from one side of her barred crib to the other, chirruping "Hi, nurse" once for each of the thirty-two freshmen. A ward of young tonsillectomy patients snoring in an ether haze, their weary, relieved mothers sitting nearby. A playroom, empty during this quiet afternoon hour. Another ward, this one nearest to the nurses' desk . . . a cardboard kitten and three pink pigs in a bright wall display . . . five cribs in a row . . . in the first one a tousle-haired tot whose large dark eyes moved from one student's face to the next, his thumb anchored mid-center of his smile. Next, blonde braids flung across her pillow, a little girl napped beside a lumpy teddybear. An empty bed and another.

At the last bed Julia's gaze followed a line of intravenous tubing from the suspended bottle of solution to the pale, still arm below. She glanced at the sleeping face below the helmet-like bandaging. Something about him made her look more closely. Little Blue Eyes, of course! Little Blue Eyes, his fright and pain hushed by sleep.

He stirred a bit, moaned, and for an instant his breathing seemed suspended.

"Mrs. Braddock!" shrilled Julia. "Is he . . . is he all right?"

The director of nurses made her way through the close-crowded freshmen, all of them staring with quick sympathy. Even as she checked the child's pulse her stern eyes turned to Julia. She gave the still-sleeping child's hand a comforting pat and led the girls out of the ward.

When they were well down the corridor and out of earshot of any of the patients, Mrs. Braddock called the group

9

to attention. "Panic is contagious, Miss Rogers. Don't make that mistake again. A good nurse keeps her heart well in hand." Her glance moved from one face to another, the firm tone of her voice giving way to a gentle one. "I am touched by the concern I see in each of your faces. You couldn't be nurses if you didn't care, but there are better ways of showing what you feel. Let your compassion show in your willingness and your gentleness. Even the youngest child can read your face—let him read confidence and cheerfulness and kindness. Your strength may be the only strength he has left."

Julia swallowed the lump in her throat and managed a wobbly smile. What a world of understanding lay beneath that sparkling white cap! Under the gold MH of her nurse's pin beat a heart large enough not only for the patients but for foolish would-be nurses, too.

The last stop on the tour was at the tiny first-floor chapel where two stained glass windows rainbowed the afternoon sunrays, one showing the Star of David and the other, the Cross of Christianity. "The chapel," explained Mrs. Braddock, "is open to patients, visitors, and hospital personnel. One of our young doctors calls this his Consultation Room. Please feel free to make it yours, too.

"Now, young ladies, your first day of training is completed. Only one thousand and ninety-four to go." Her brown eyes swept their faces again. "Much will be asked of you because you, each of you, has much to give."

Julia felt taller, more responsible than ever before.

2

A Handful of Water

The brain is a mass of some 12,000,000,000 cells and the freshmen soon came to believe that Mercy Hospital School of Nursing was bent on presenting a minimum of one fact per cell.

Mornings were spent in the hospital classrooms where the art of nursing was taught and practiced. Taking temperatures (their own), taking blood pressures (each other's) while trying to remember the name of the blood pressure machine and how to spell it (sphygmomanometer), practising bath-giving on a human-sized doll named Mary Chase, learning to make beds with corners mitered, sheets taut, and learning to give hypodermics (first practice shots were injected into a grapefruit) . . . for each one procedure learned, five more to be learned.

"What I have is cranium strainium," complained red-headed Lois Evans on the bus back from afternoon classes at Mercy College. "And if I have to carry these books much longer I'll have interrupted circulation, too. In case you don't know, the combined weight of Microbiology, Anatomy, Pharmacology and Diet Therapy is eight pounds and eleven ounces!"

"Oh, please," groaned Rosemary, from across the aisle. "Not another number to remember. Two hundred and six bones, twelve cranial nerves, five million red blood cells, five thousand white blood cells. I am numb with numbers."

Julia laughed. "Lois, for a girl who's dating nine fellows I'd say your circulation is in great shape."

Pretending insult Lois said, "Sociology is the study of human relations and I just happen to be—"

"A dedicated scholar," Lou Ellen Archer concluded. "But why limit your research to blond basketball players? There are other generations and, for that matter, another gender. If you spent a little time around the dorm you'd find a wide assortment of types to study."

"Dandy," Lois retorted. "I could watch Julia write to Paul, or Rosemary divide and conquer her nightly pizza or better yet, I could watch you, Archer . . . a study of the human mind blotting up page after page of texts so you can give us your daily demonstration of braininess."

Lou Ellen arched one eyebrow and smiled sweetly. "It's a matter of choosing which to exercise—mind or mouth."

Rosemary called a halt. "We are on a public bus, gals, and we are student nurses and we do have some responsibility to the profession." She unwrapped a chocolate bar. "Anyway, you two are giving me nervous nerves and when I get upset I get hungry. If I end up weighing two hundred pounds you'll be responsible!" The candy bar disappeared in three quick bites.

"Sorry, Rosie." Lois grinned and nudged Lou Ellen. "From now on we'll keep you so calm we'll have to call you Skinny."

"And when your nerves are thoroughly soothed," Lou Ellen added, "we'll change your name to Elizabeth and call you Tranquil-lizza."

The moans of laughter were a welcome sound to Julia.

12

The tension of seven weeks of concentration showed in many of the girls' faces. "You know what's wrong with us?" she asked, addressing no one in particular. "We're theory-weary." Over the choresed groans she went on, "No, I'm serious. My head is stuffed with the art and science of nursing but we might as well be a million miles from a hospital. What I want to do is soothe the fevered brow of a genuine patient."

The last few blocks of the bus ride were spent in silence, each girl mentally placing herself at a hospital bedside, each one wishing for and dreading the moment when she would answer the call, "Nurse."

Julia checked her mail slot and pushed the disappointment of no-letter-again to the back of her mind. Nine days of no-letter . . . longer than ever before. Of course, Paul was busy. He would write oftener if he had more time. Boot camp was nearly over and then he'd have time for more than a quick two pages once a week. Then her mail slot would cease to be "cobweb corners." As she climbed the stairs toward the third floor, she stopped at the second floor landing to watch the late afternoon fog roll in from the ocean. San Francisco fog. Except for a Saturday afternoon of bicycling in Golden Gate park and the Sunday her family drove up for a day-long picnic at Fleishhaker Zoo, she'd seen almost nothing of the city. "A hermit" Rosemary called her but she had decided to save San Francisco to see with Paul. Paul. Paul. Paul. Why don't you write, write, write!

"Rogers!"

Julia turned at the sound of her name. "Oh, hi, Miss Lambert."

"How's my little sister?"

"Fine," replied Julia, her glance moving as it always did from Sue Lambert's face to the white cap with its junior

13

class stripe perched atop her brown curls. "I'm fine, big sister."

"You're not, but you will be. If your fellow would remember to mark Student Nurse after your name it would help. This got mixed in with the patients' mail." Sue held out a letter, THE letter.

Julia stared at the beautiful scrawl that was Paul's. She slipped the letter into her Diet Therapy book. "Thanks a lot, Sue . . . I mean Miss Lambert."

"No, no—no need to be so formal unless you're getting in practice for tomorrow."

"What's tomorrow?"

"You haven't seen the bulletin board? You start floor duty tomorrow. You're going to be on Third Floor Surgical, with me."

A swell of excitement filled the first floor and echoed up the stairs as the news spread. Voices babbled and shrilled, swallowing up Julia's own breathless tumble of questions.

Floor duty . . . tomorrow! Like the tide, the freshmen's self-confidence crested and ebbed. Yesterday they were sure they were ready. Now they were equally sure they were not. Through supper, the two-hour compulsory study period, and all the long evening the only topic of conversation was floor duty. Occasionally an upperclassman stopped by the crowded little kitchen, talk headquarters, to wish them well. One or two stayed to tell of horrible or hilarious first-day experiences. No one studied, no one went down to the recreation room for television, no one gave a moment's thought to any subject other than tomorrow's assignment. "Medical —I would be sent to medical. What if I'm giving a bath and he has a heart attack right in the middle—" "in the middle of his chest, that's where he'd have a heart attack, goofy." "Or suppose you're feeding a patient and he chokes. What would you do?" "I'd call a nurse." "But you're the

14

nurse!" "Who me? Well, in that case, I'd call the bus station." "For what?" "For a reservation home." "No, seriously, what would you do?" On and on went the whirl of words, each girl contributing to the imaginary emergencies they might face, each sure that tomorrow would be her last day in the profession. At "lights out" the conversational what-ifs gave way to a tense quiet. Suddenly Julia leaped from bed and fumbled for the light switch.

Rosemary moaned, "It's too early to start getting dressed now, Julia."

"I forgot all about it, Rosie. I put it in one of my books and I forgot all about it."

"Thirty-two girls and I had to room with the addled one." Rosemary blinked against the flare of light. "What are you doing, Julia? Studying now is as hopeless as studying for an I.Q. test."

"Diet Therapy. Where is my Diet Therapy book?"

"If you insist on this madness, use mine."

"The letter is in *my book*, not yours. Paul's letter."

"Well, you've read it about forty times."

"Not this one. It came today and in all the excitement I forgot about it. I would like to read it now. If you really want to be helpful you'll quit arguing and help me find my Diet Therapy book."

Rosemary yawned and flung back the covers. "When do I get to meet this marvel of a man, he who keeps my life in turmoil, he who costs me sleep on the night before my debut to the world of painful pain, he who—"

"If you 'he who' one more time I'll—never mind, here it is." She flung the text aside, ripped open the fragile envelope and, eyes racing across the single page, began to smile. "He'll be home tomorrow, *tomorrow*. Oh, Rosie, he'll be home TOMORROW!"

"Home where? Home here?"

15

"No, silly, home. San Dorcas."

"Gee, that's nice. You'll only be a hundred miles apart instead of five hundred."

"Why, I'll go home."

"Sure you will—Saturday. You were going home then anyway for Betsy's wedding. But this is Tuesday and we have several thousand baths to give between now and then. You won't be going anywhere if we're caught with the lights on, so let's get some sleep."

Julia read the letter one more time, turned off the light and crawled into bed. "Know what, Rosie?"

"What?"

"The human mind is quite limited."

"Like how?"

"It can only worry about one thing at a time. For the last ten minutes I haven't been a bit concerned about going on floor duty tomorrow."

"Thanks, Julia, thanks a lot. For a minute there I was getting drowsy."

At six-fifty A.M. Julia stepped from the elevator into the dim corridor of BIII. She took a deep breath, pressed her hand to the nervous knot perched atop her breakfast, and walked toward the glow of light that must be the nurses' station. Four nurses stood silhouetted in light and shadow. Her heart pounded as she moved along on jelly legs.

A light flashed over an open doorway and a faint buzz sounded at the nurses' station. One figure moved to answer the patient's signal.

A white-clad graduate stepped toward Julia. "Miss Rogers?"

Julia nodded.

"I'm Mrs. Proctor, surgical ward instructor. This is Miss

Underwood, floor supervisor. And Miss Lambert will be your team leader. Oh, here's Miss Lambert and you must be Miss Archer." As more introductions were made Julia glanced at Lou Ellen Archer, but found no sign of anxiety in her placid half-smile.

Miss Underwood said, "We're ready for report now. Miss Rogers, Miss Archer, please listen carefully. You'll be given your assignments as soon as the report is completed. The condition of your patients during the night will have a bearing on the care they will require this morning. Miss Wilson, we'll begin with your patients."

Senior student Vicky Wilson, alert in spite of her tiredness, flicked the first card of the patient file. "Room 301, Mrs. Martin. Dr. McGill's appendectomy. Second day post op. Mrs. Martin had a fairly good night. She has an order for Morphine Sulphate grain 1/6 every four hours if needed, which was given last at 2 A.M. She slept from 2:30 until about 6. She is voiding. She goes on soft diet this A.M."

"Room 302, Bed 1, Mr. Hogan, Dr. Gordani's patient admitted last night for plastic repair of burn scars right arm for OR at eight. Pre op medications given as ordered. Surgery permit signed and his chart is ready."

The terse report continued, bed by bed, patient by patient, until Miss Wilson's twelve patients were accounted for. Then Mrs. Stamper, R.N., reported her twelve charges and senior student Amy Walton reported on those in her care. In each voice Julia heard an undercurrent of concern, a compassion that was the heartbeat of nursing.

But nursing is also doing and the doing was soon underway. "Here are your assignments, girls. You have three baths to complete before 9:30. Breakfast trays are coming up now. Miss Vaughn, the senior from the diet kitchen, will check each tray for accuracy."

Julia watched the big tray cart roll down the hall toward her, only the tip of tiny Miss Vaughn's cap visible above the rubber-wheeled vehicle.

Suppose I spill a tray or take it to the wrong patient. Suppose you quit talking to yourself and pay attention to business.

"Room 305, Bed 3, Mr. Durbell. Soft diet," chirped Miss Vaughn, extending a tray in Julia's direction.

Julia froze.

Lou Ellen reached for it, gave the name card a cursory glance as if to double check the diet senior, and skimmed down the hall toward 305.

Julia's mouth was cotton dry as she said, "I'll take the next one."

"Room 303, Bed 1, Mr. Daskalu. Diabetic diet."

As one patient after another greeted her with unusually cheerful hellos Julia realized that first-day-of-duty was an event for the patients as well as the freshmen. Trays served. Trays returned to the cart. Everything ticking along precisely.

Seven-fifty-three . . . the O.R. gurney with Mr. Hogan aboard moved into the elevator steered by two turbaned surgical technicians.

Julia felt the bath assignment paper in her apron pocket and her newfound confidence shattered. Sue Lambert paused to wink encouragement as she accompanied a doctor making rounds.

The assignment sheet was almost as informative as morning report. "Mrs. Humboldt, Room 307, Right nephrectomy." Let's see. That's a kidney operation. "Seventh day post. op." Oh, good, she'll be over most of the soreness. "Up in chair T.I.D." Three times a day. Wonderful! I can change her bed while she's in the chair. This is going to be easy.

18

Easy it was. Mrs. Humboldt chatted about her grand-children, her lawyer son, her rose garden, and the novel she was reading. Julia felt graduate-efficient as she helped her first patient back between the smooth sweet-smelling sheets. Ward Instructor Mrs. Proctor entered the room in time to see the patient settle back against the plumped-up pillows.

"Very good, Miss Rogers. Only 8:20 and you've completed your first bath." Her smile stiffened as her eyes moved to the heap of linen on the floor. "The linen cart, Miss Rogers."

"Yes, Mrs. Proctor."

Mrs. Humboldt bristled a bit. "This child gives a lovely bath and she's patient as can be with a rattle-tongued old lady. Couldn't you forgive the breach of laundry regulations?"

Mrs. Proctor laughed. "With you as a defense attorney Miss Rogers could almost get away with tossing the bath water out the window."

The next patient, Mr. Amchek, Room 309, Bed 2, took longer. Julia picked up the toothpowder can instead of the talcum and liberally sprinkled the grainy powder in preparation for the backrub. This required a second back washing and the hands of her watch raced with her as she tried to make up lost time. This patient was confined to bed rest and the sheets, so easy to smooth on an empty bed, were a tangled mass under Julia's unskilled hands. By turning the patient from side to side, not once but twice, over the hump of clean linen, pushed to the center of the bed to meet yesterday's sheets, she finally finished.

"This is the most exercise I've had in a week," puffed the wizened old man as Julia tucked blankets and mitered the corners with a satisfing geometric neatness. "Mind you, I'm not complaining about the Easter egg rolling you gave

19

me but I would appreciate it if you'd loosen the top covers, Miss. I can't move my toes at all, at all."

Julia flushed as she saw the old gentleman's feet bound down tight by her too well-made corners.

Linen safely deposited in the hall laundry cart, all that remained was the disposal of the bath water. The bathroom was occupied by the other patient so Julia, anxious to get to the last bath of her assignment, decided to empty the stainless steel bowl in the utility room hopper down the hall. Hurrying, she stepped into the corridor and into a head-on collision with a white uniformed doctor. Bath water drenched doctor, floor and Julia.

Julia clung to the basin and watched in stunned silence as the doctor cupped his hand to catch the last drips from his chin.

With a ridiculous caution against spilling, he emptied the handful of water into the bath basin.

In an instant the corridor seemed to come alive with people and the sight of the dripping resident physician seemed to fracture everyone's funnybone . . . except Julia's. Her face aflame, she stammered apologies. He answered that this was an annual occurrence.

Mrs. Braddock brought towels. Mrs. Proctor sent Miss Lambert for a maid and a mop. A doctor making rounds with Miss Underwood laughingly suggested that Dr. Johnson take his shower in a less public place.

Dr. Johnson remarked on the cruelty of laughing at a drowning man and walked away, each step a squish.

Julia was doing a good job of the mop-up until a smiling Lou Ellen stopped to tell Mrs. Proctor that her assignments were finished. Julia's anger at herself and the mess she'd made brought a spill of tears, a salty contribution to the puddle.

Mrs. Proctor laid a comforting hand on her shoulder.

"Accidents happen, Miss Rogers, even to the most efficient. You run over to your room and change so you won't be late to class. I'll assign your last bath to another nurse." With a grin she confided, "My first collision was with . . . well, it wasn't with bath water!"

Back in her room Julia wiggled free of the cold, clinging uniform. With trembling fingers she slipped clips through button shanks of a fresh uniform. Her eyes smarted and her head ached. Nine-twenty-five. In another hour Paul would be home. How easy it would be to pack and run. Paul would welcome her with open arms. Three wonderful weeks with Paul . . . and then what? Marriage? Marriage, the aspirin you take for the headache of failure?

The dressing table mirror reflected a total absence of makeup and birds-nest hair. Julia looked herself in her mirrored eyes. You have 12,000,000,000 brain cells. Surely one of them can figure a way to empty a basin without engulfing a doctor!

At ten to ten Rosemary came in to pick up her books. "Lou Ellen's telling everyone you gave *four* baths this morning. Did you?"

"Well, yes." Julia giggled, mentally ticking off her two bed baths and two hall showers. "In a way I did."

"And she says you managed to meet that darling Dr. Johnson!"

"Yes, yes I did."

"Boy, Julia, you have all the luck."

3

Mercy to Montezuma

Friday 5 P.M.—the moment etched itself in Julia's memory. She had almost forgotten the strength of Paul's embrace but Friday at 5 P.M. she gasped for breath as his uniformed arms lifted and whirled her about in the center of the nurses' living room. His fifteen weeks of rugged training, her fifteen weeks of loneliness came to an end in the dizzy delight of his powerful hug. For a moment she thought she had a cracked rib or two and her heart seemed to swell far beyond the confines of her blue angora sweater. "Oh, Paul," she whispered. "Oh, Paul!"

Rosemary, strolling in with Julia's overnight case, said, "I take it this is a friend of yours."

When she could get her breath, Julia said, "Rosie, I want you to meet Paul Hammond. Paul, this is my roommate, Rosemary Dowling."

Paul nodded acknowledgment but the wisps of blue angora clinging to his dark green uniform demanded most of his attention. "We'd better get in gear, Julia. Glad to meet you, Rosemary."

"Not so fast, Private." Rosemary inspected him like a top sergeant, from his mirror-bright shoes to his G.I. haircut.

"You're right, Julia. He is a healthy American male. He's not eight feet tall as I'd been led to believe and his lips are a bit flushed but I guess that's healthy American girl lipstick."

A smile climbed freckle by freckle to Julia's eyes. "For only eight weeks of nurse's training you are extremely accurate in your observations, Miss Dowling. If we weren't in such a hurry I'd let you check his pulse, too."

Anxiously Paul reached for the suitcase. "Let's go, Julia. We've got some mileage to make. The bachelor dinner for Phil is at seven-thirty."

Rosemary grinned. "I packed your Microbiology book, Julia, so you can spend the weekend studying for Monday's test."

"Come on, Julia."

"Bye, Rosie!"

Ten minutes later Julia rushed in the nurses' home door. "I forgot to sign out and Paul's not at all happy that I insisted on coming back. Oh, Rosie, why didn't you remind me? That's what roommates are for!"

Fifty-three hours later Julia signed in, exhausted by the frantic pace of the weekend. Rosemary was already asleep and Julia crawled into her own bed hoping her tangled thoughts would give way to sleep. But weariness alone could not account for the confusion of her feelings.

The Psychology lecturer's words from her Friday afternoon class came back to her: *To understand your patients you must first understand yourself.* Clearly she did not understand herself. *Analyze your emotions.* Where to begin?

Weariness was hardly an emotion but she did realize how helpful was the routine of her nursing school life—and how good it felt to be home at Mercy again. Home? Why, home was San Dorcas. No, home was Mercy, now. The thought gave her an uneasy feeling of disloyalty to her family.

Her family—how ashamed she felt that she had managed so little time with them this weekend. She should have spent a weekend with them before Paul came home. Aside from the two hours Paul had been at the Friday night bachelor dinner she had shared every waking minute with him. And if Paul's home were not right next door she would have seen even less of her family. Paul could talk of little but the Marine Corps. John had listened with fourteen-year-old's absorption. Walter and Mary Rogers had listened politely and patiently, making occasional efforts to turn the conversation to Julia's new world. But Paul's enthusiasm for the Corps could not be stalled. Julia listened, loving the sound of his voice, admiring the new note of authority in it. Mike had listened for a while but a little of Paul was enough for him. With a seven-year-old's directness he had asked, "Mama, when is Julia coming home to see us?"

How Paul had laughed at that. "I believe I have a rival, Julia. I think your kid brother is jealous."

Jealousy. The word had skimmed her thinking a hundred times this weekend. Now, in the darkness of her dormitory room she opened the door of her mind and let the ugly word out. Jealous. I'm jealous of the Marine Corps. From the halls of Montezuma to the shores of Tripoli. How silly! How could she be jealous of a whole branch of the U.S. military? She was, and the knowledge that jealousy was a childish emotion, rooted in selfishness, sent a chill through her. Thinking back, she realized how certain she'd been that Paul would press for an early marriage. He was home for twenty days leave and with the solemn beauty of Betsy and Phil's wedding to set the mood she had expected Paul to insist on setting a date. She was prepared with twenty reasons why they should wait. The sight of

24

Betsy in slipper satin and lacy veil had weakened Julia's resolve but the appropriate moment for Paul's plea came and went without the slightest mention of marriage—not even when he kissed her goodnight at the nurses' home door.

Paul acted like a man in love all right—but in love with the whole bloomin' Marine Corps. The "we" of his conversation referred to the fellows of his squad. When she'd told him of her bath water–everywhere episode she'd expected him to laugh, but he'd said in all seriousness, "You'd never make a Marine, Julia. Poor coordination." And because of his verdict she felt she'd failed him somehow. She'd made it through her own sort of boot camp, hadn't she? Two girls had gone home but she was still at Mercy, still trying. She hadn't spilled any more bath water, had she? She had broken a thermometer on Thursday, but the slippery thing had practically leaped from her hand.

A flicker of moonlight caught her attention and brought her back to the purpose of all this thought. *Analyze the motivation to understand the action.* Obviously Paul was as caught up in his new life as she was in hers. Nothing wrong with that. Nothing, except the tiny area of hurt around her heart. Viewed sensibly, there was no cause for pain. Paul was now mature enough to see the wisdom of waiting. With strong sure love he was, in effect, freeing her to concentrate on her nursing. They hadn't talked much about her profession, in fact he hadn't allowed her much conversation at all. But now that she had analyzed the situation she understood Paul, and herself, far better.

Psychology, the study of human behavior and its motivation. Only eight weeks of psychology and see how expertly, how easily she had determined Paul's motives. A nurse's education offered some splendid by-products. Bless you, Mercy. And you, too, Mr. Montezuma.

4

Doctor Ma

October went by in a rush. Three of the weekends were spent in San Dorcas, mostly because of Paul's leave but she was careful to include time for her family. The Julia Rogers Self-Analysis-and-Right-Mental-Attitude course saw her through many hours of Marine Corps history and boot camp difficulties, told and retold until she knew every Gung Ho! episode by heart.

The demanding schedule of studies and floor duty went on. Every day brought new patients and each day Julia felt a bit more at ease. The patient bath was a procedure she knew well and performed well, although the morning Mr. Hepple lost his dentures in the sheets convinced her that no procedure was totally routine. After a month of BIII she knew every patient by name, diagnosis, and room number. Most of them were likable but even the unpleasant ones were due the same quality of nursing care. She watched her first patient, Mrs. Humboldt, gain strength with each passing day and, when time for her discharge came, Julia felt a sense of pride at her small part in this woman's recovery.

Discharges meant empty beds, beds to be cleaned and

remade with fresh sheets, and utensils to be sterilized. Room 307 which yesterday was Mrs. Humboldt's was now Mrs. Tarrington's and Julia soon regretted the change.

In the kitchen Julia scooped up ice for the thermos marked 307. "What a witch," she complained.

"Who?" asked Sue Lambert as she topped Mr. Walden's eggnog with a sprinkle of nutmeg.

"Mrs. Tarrington, that's who. Through the whole admittance—temperature, blood pressure, clothes check—she snapped at me. I can diagnose her: short temper, sharp tongue."

"Those are symptoms, Rogers, not the cause. Go read her chart and you'll change your thinking considerably."

When her new patient was finally settled and she had a minute to spare Julia followed Miss Lambert's advice.

Alice Tarrington Age 38
Admitted for transfusion of whole blood, diagnostic X-rays, and biopsy of underarm lump. Family history of malignancy.

So that was it—fear. Mrs. Tarrington's sharpness was a defense. Anemia had sapped the strength she might have had to face this ordeal so she chose harsh words to prevent any show of sympathy, sympathy which would reduce her to tears.

Understanding was the key to Mrs. Tarrington, Julia realized, and an older, wiser nurse had put this key in her hand. Sue Lambert, only one year more experienced, knew how to look beneath the surface complaints. With Sue's help, Julia took a giant step forward.

The Assignment sheet was posted on the bulletin board each week. By mid-November Julia was so accustomed to

27

finding her name under BIII she barely glanced at the sheet. But today her name was not there. Anxiously her eyes searched the roster and stopped at AI East, Male Medical Wards. She knew BIII and liked BIII. She didn't want to leave . . . with a smile at her foolishness she moved aside so other girls could check their assignments. Before she graduated she would know every inch of Mercy Hospital from the diet kitchen and supply rooms in the basement to the top floor operating rooms. BIII was one step, AI East was another, and there would be many, many more.

Friday, December twenty-first was a gray drizzling day and a long day for Julia. Classes were suspended for two weeks and the freshmen had week-long holidays. While one half the class vacationed, the other half worked full eight-hour shifts. Julia's parents would pick her up when she got off duty at noon Monday, Christmas eve. She could hardly wait! A sudden swell of homesickness had engulfed her during the traditional caroling Thursday evening, a candlelit procession of students moving through each darkened corridor, offering their gift of song to the patients. Christmas was a time to be home. She would be home Monday but until then, there were two sprawling wards on AI East, every bed occupied, each man in need of nursing care.

At two-forty-five Julia made final check of each of her six patients. Mr. Tipton, new patient, sleeping now after a tiring morning of X-rays; Mr. Carpenter, cheerfully exaggerating his illness to his visitors; Mr. Gorgas, holding his wife's hand and assuring her that it was only a little heart attack; Mr. Cleveland, asking for water and reminding her to mark down how much, since his Intake and Output were measured; Mr. Willard, complaining as usual, because nothing ever suited Mr. Willard; and finally, dear Mr. Antoine, the curtains drawn at either side of his bed to allow him

28

some uninterrupted rest. Dear Mr. Antoine, not a tooth in his smile, his sense of humor unfailing in spite of his frail weary old body with all its ills. How disappointed he would be when he learned he would not be home for Christmas. He had watched the holiday decorations go up in the ward, opened his cards, and enjoyed the Girl Scout decorations on his dinner tray. But he continued to announce that he'd be home for Christmas. The ominous diagnosis on his chart and the zigzag of his temperature graph told Julia he'd be on AI East for a long time, weeks or months. "My little nurse girl" he called her. For a moment she wished she would be here on Christmas day to ease his disappointment.

When the change of shift report was completed and AI East was turned over to the three to eleven nurses, Julia swung her navy blue cape over her uniform and headed for the nurses' home. The day-long rain had dwindled to a mist but a chilly wind whipped at her cape. An ambulance wailed in the distance and Julia wondered where this patient would find room. There'd be beds in the halls if the accident rate continued. By Christmas there might well be "no room at the inn."

Julia and a young man in a gray topcoat reached the nurses' home entry at the same time. He opened the door against the sharp wind and followed her into the foyer. The door whipped shut with a resounding bang.

"Sorry," he said, his apology as much in his eyes as in his voice. "I hope no one is sleeping."

Julia felt uneasy under his steady gaze. "Oh, no, the night nurses are down. I mean up. Awake, that's the word."

"I'm here for Lou Ellen Archer." His brown eyes did not move from hers. "Would you be kind enough to tell her Troy's waiting?"

"Certainly." Julia motioned toward the living room. "Make yourself comfortable. I'll tell her."

29

As she mounted the stairs she mumbled, "Leave it to Lou Ellen to snag the best looking man in town and have him home for Christmas. Wish Paul were home now . . . Paul, oh darn, I forgot to check the mail!"

Lou Ellen stood at the top of the stairs, a cashmere topper slung over a ski sweater and black stretch pants. "The little men in white coats are going to haul you away, Rogers. You're talking to yourself and that's the first sign."

"I wouldn't be talking to myself if I had a six-foot-two dream waiting for me. Troy, he said."

"Some dream." Lou Ellen shrugged. "If you want him I'll wrap him up and give him to you for Christmas. To me he's mere transportation." She continued down the stairs, asked casually, "Are you coming to our open house Sunday? Mom and Dad invited the whole class, you know."

"Thanks, Lou Ellen. I'll try." To herself she added, If I didn't have a fellow, I'd take you up on your first offer. A nice young man like Troy deserves better treatment than "mere transportation."

Sunday began with bright clear sunshine but by eight o'clock Julia was no longer aware of the sun-flooded windows of AI East. Since morning report at seven she had checked Mr. Antoine at ten-minute intervals. Twice she had called the supervisor to his bedside. The second time Mrs. Bolton said, "A cool sponge might help bring his temperature down, Miss Rogers. Dr. Turner will be in shortly." While the other students served breakfast trays, Julia filled a basin with tepid water. As soon as she returned to his bedside Mr. Antoine roused.

"Miss Rogers."

"Yes, Mr. Antoine." Her fingers felt out the weak pulse in his wrist. "Yes?"

In a thin, tired voice he whispered, "Merry Christmas, my little nurse girl."

Julia bit her tongue to keep from correcting him. Christmas was two days away, but confusion in one so ill, one so old was not unusual.

His faded blue eyes looked at her from deep shadows, his skin pinched and tight. His limp hand reached out in an appealing gesture.

Julia clasped the crooked bony fingers in both her hands. "What is it, Mr. Antoine? Can I get you something?"

The shake of his head was almost imperceptible. He clutched at her fingers. She responded with gentle pressure. He relaxed, his sigh a moan.

"Don't go. You please stay . . . with me."

Julia glanced at the patients nearby but they busied themselves with their breakfasts, refusing to meet her eyes. Uneasiness swept through her. All the other students were serving trays in Ward B. Should she ask Mr. Willard in the next bed to ring for the supervisor? No, she had her instructions, and Dr. Turner would be in soon.

"Of course I'll stay with you, Mr. Antoine." Her steady voice did not betray her mounting alarm. "I'll just sponge your face." She tried to remove her fingers from his grip, but he clung tightly.

"You please stay. Not long, little nurse girl . . ." his voice faltered, ". . . not long." The strength of his fingers crumbled to helplessness. His eyes gently closed.

"Mr. Antoine! Mr. Antoine!" The words screamed through her mind but, spoken, were a prayerful whisper.

His eyes opened a slit. "You . . . nice . . . nurse girl," he managed and his eyes closed for the last time.

Julia couldn't quell the strangling in her throat. She had to walk the length of the ward, past the other patients, down

31

the long corridor to the nurses' station. She must be calm, deliberate. She must not cry and she must not scream the words that whirled a panic path from her head to her heart. Mr. Antoine is dead.

"Mr. Antoine is dead."

The supervisor gave no reply, but she made a hurried trip to the ward and the moment she returned to the desk, picked up the phone.

"Did you hear me, Mrs. Bolton?" Julia's eyes brimmed. "Mr. Antoine—"

"I heard you, Miss Rogers. I'm calling the resident doctor. It's a doctor, not a nurse, who pronounces a patient's expiration." She spoke into the phone, then turned back to Julia. "You'd better sit down."

Julia covered her mouth with rigid fingers as though to down the hurt in her throat. "It was . . . such a . . . shock."

"Death is always a shock, Miss Rogers, always." Mrs. Bolton offered her a glass of water and insisted she drink it.

"Thank you, Mrs. Bolton. I'm all right now."

With these words Julia put into action all the self-discipline she'd learned in five months of training. Even for death there was a standard hospital procedure, beginning with the doctor's vain attempt to find a heartbeat and ending with the final sign-off of the patient's chart. And there was much else to do, baths, treatments, lunch trays, noon temperatures, and a hundred other demands. Through all the long day Julia wore a tight-lipped smile to camouflage the cold weight that grew and grew in her chest.

When the black hands of the hall clock finally pointed to three, Julia was too numb to feel relief. It wasn't until she had traded uniform for bathrobe and had thrown herself across her bed that she loosed the rein on her emotions. But her sobs were dry and tears would not come.

Mr. Antoine is dead. No, nurses say "expired." "Expired"

32

sounds like a forgotten magazine subscription. Expired. Dead. Gone. Home for Christmas, he'd said and believed. I wish I were home. I wish Mom were here. I wish . . .

Julia pounded her pillow with futile fists, angry at the cruelty of death, at her own failure. She was a failure. Good nurses don't . . . ache so.

A light knock on the door brought Julia suddenly up-right, and she pulled her robe tight around her to stop shivering.

"Yes?"

Ma Marsh opened the door and stepped inside. "Miss Dowling's not here?"

"No, Ma. She had first vacation." Julia knew Ma hadn't climbed two flights of stairs to ask what the signout book could answer. Ma was slow on the stairs, less because of her years than her pillow-like plumpness.

"And you're off duty now?"

"Yes, I got off at three."

"Then why aren't you dressing for Open House at the Archers? It started at four, you know."

"I'm not going." Julia felt Ma's eyes on her disheveled hair, her pinched, unconvincing smile. "I have to pack and I have to do some studying and Paul might call and—"

"You can pack in ten minutes and classes are suspended for the holidays and I'll have the call transferred if he phones. Get dressed. There's a map on the bulletin board so you'll find your way with no trouble. Come on, Miss Rogers, get started."

"But I don't feel like a party."

"Julia, it isn't always what we feel like doing that counts. A nurse who has no social life is. . . ." She searched for the right word. ". . . is lopsided."

"But, Ma. . . ."

"No buts! You stayed home from the Halloween and

33

Thanksgiving dances. I want you to go to that Open House. The eight-block walk to the Archers will be good for—for your complexion." She stepped over Julia's crumpled uniform, opened the closet door and pulled out a red wool. "This will be fine. I'll give you exactly twenty minutes to get dressed and sign out."

Julia walked four blocks in the crisp evening air before she realized Ma Marsh hadn't mentioned Mr. Antoine. Ma Marsh never pried, but she knew more from the nurses' kitchen conversation than she ever let on. She pretends not to know your troubles and then pretends authority to order a solution. The old fraud, the dear, stern, motherly old fraud. Ma Marsh's prescription for heartache: a party. Well, it was a good try, Dr. Ma, but it won't help a bit.

5

Wish I May, Wish I Might

Colored lights and a giant wreath with a shiny red bow marked the Archers' doorway. Julia rang the bell and wondered if it would be heard over the confusion of voices within. Sudden laughter burst out. She turned to go, to run from this dreadful gaiety, but before she could make good her escape, the massive door swung back. A young man handsomely decked out in dark tweeds, a red vest, and wreath green tie said, "Well, hello to you, Julie Rogers!"

A name, a vague elusive name flicked through her mind. "Oh, you're Troy," she said at last. Lou Ellen's mere transportation was now apparently reduced to mere doorman. "I didn't expect to see you."

"Why not? I live here. Didn't old loupy Lou tell you— I'm her brother. Come in, Julie." He extended a warm hand to draw her inside.

"Her brother," Julia laughed, as she mentally assigned new motives and friendlier adjectives to Lou Ellen. She stepped into the hallway and her breath caught in surprised appreciation. Golden oak paneling swept upward to a vaulted ceiling, a carpeted stairway circled into the darkness of the upper story. "How lovely!"

"Do you like old houses?" Troy asked, taking her coat, his smile approving her red wool sheath dress.

"Oh, yes—and this one's beautiful." Her eyes shone like the prisims of the chandelier in the stairwell.

"Next time I'll give you a guided tour, but you're missing the party." Troy led her to the longest living room she had ever seen, so big that the forty or more people did not crowd it. He introduced Julia to his parents, Judge and Mrs. Archer, and began further introductions.

When the door chime sounded again Lou Ellen came over. "Will you get the door, Troy? Martha's still busy serving eggnog. I'll introduce Julia around."

The next minutes were a blur of names and faces. Julia said hello to several girls of her freshman class and met a more than equal number of young men, thoughtfully provided by Lou Ellen. For a moment Julia was caught up in the light mood of the party. They moved to another group for introductions.

"Eggnog or punch?" offered a uniformed maid. "Miss Lou Ellen, your mama wants you in the kitchen, please." Lou Ellen excused herself and left.

Julia found herself with no words and a smile that felt pasted in place. Her hand clutching an eggnog, she timidly moved away from the conversation groups and sat down on the bench of the grand piano at the far end of the room. She sipped eggnog and its coldness seeped through her. Someone suggested carols, and she moved to make room for the volunteer pianist.

"It came upon a midnight clear. . . ."

The old ache came back to her throat and she could not sing. She studied the majestic white Christmas tree flood-lighted in the bay window. The sparkling ornaments were a rich blue green, precisely the same shade as Lou Ellen's dress. Too modern for the stately old house, too decorator-

36

perfect to suggest a family's enjoyment, the tree depressed her.

"I'm dreaming of a white Christmas. . . ."

The song with its undertone of melancholy made the lights, the bright room swim in a lens of tears. Her one thought was escape. She backed away from the crowd around the piano. The hallway and freedom seemed miles away. Back, back, a wall stopped her. Frantically looking about she found a closed door. A door to somewhere, anywhere. She turned the knob, slipped through and closed the door, leaning against it, grateful for the quiet and the darkness. As she groped for a handkerchief she felt pressure against the door.

"Julie! Julie!"

She stepped forward in the darkness. A light flared on the far side of the room, its glow illuminating a desk, a leather chair, and book-lined walls.

Troy came toward her. "Is something wrong, Julia? Silly question. Of course something's wrong."

"I . . . I don't want . . . this eggnog."

He reached for the crystal cup with an amused grin. "Just don't tell my father. It's his prize recipe."

Julia tried to smile, but a sob broke from her chest.

"Holy Moses!" Troy rubbed nervous fingers through his dark hair. He led Julia to a leather couch before a fireplace. Easing her down on the cushions, he said, "Okay, cry it out. You couldn't stop now if you tried."

Turning to the fireplace he laid paper, kindling, and two logs. At the touch of a match it flared. Sitting back on his heels, he patted her hand. "Feeling better?" He pressed a handkerchief into her hands. "Do you want to tell me about it?"

Julia tried but his kindness brought forth new tears.

Troy grimaced, moved to the couch beside her, and mumbled, "Opportunity, you can quit knocking. Even I am bright enough to know when a shoulder is needed." He slid his arm around her and tucked her blonde head under his chin.

Julia yielded to the comfort of his rough tweeds and tender strength. When her tears were spent she said, "I'm sorry, Troy."

"Don't be," he soothed. "Why don't you tell me about it?"

Somewhere in the room a clock ticked. Minutes went by but there was no urgency in Troy's manner. She struggled to find words that could explain. Once begun, it was easy to tell him of her deep attachment for old Mr. Antoine and how badly she felt because he couldn't go home for Christmas.

Troy did not speak at once. She felt his chest rise with a deep breath. "I'm surprised at you, Julie. Mr. Antoine did go home. I have a hunch he knew he was dying. Home isn't always a street address, you know."

She mulled this new thought. "Maybe. But I wanted to help him get well." Her hands twisted the damp handkerchief. "The object of nursing is to help people get well."

"You're partly right. But when getting well isn't possible a nurse has another task—giving comfort, helping the patient meet death."

The fire crackled, a log rolled forward on the iron grate and a shower of sparks danced upward.

Troy laughed self-consciously. "Listen to me making speeches. I'm in my second year of law and already I think I'm Clarence Darrow."

Julia shifted, toed off her shoes, and curled her feet beside her. "You've helped me a lot, Troy."

"Medicine is like law, in a way. Always a new dimension

38

to be understood. There's nothing thin or flat about justice. My father tried to explain this to me but I think you have to be a part of a profession before you begin to understand its depths."

"I like nursing, but I'm not sure I'll ever be a good nurse. How will anyone be able to lean on me when my knees are so rubbery?"

Troy chuckled. "That can be a good quality. A person who is rubbery will bounce back. Heaven help the rigid type. They're brittle and they break."

Julia watched a tiny flame turn from red to blue, then wane to a steady gold. "You're a nice guy, Troy Archer," she said softly. "You're missing a very nice party just to console me."

His arm tightened, pressing her close enough to hear the rhythmic pulsing of her heart. "My pleasure, Miss Rogers. Besides, this is the most obvious answer to my prayer I've ever had."

She leaned away to look at him. "You're teasing me!"

"I am not. Settle back and I'll prove it." When she did, he began, husky-voiced, "Lord make me an instrument of Thy peace. Where there is hatred, let me sow love. Where there is injury, pardon. Where there is doubt, faith. Where there is despair, hope. Where there is darkness, light. Where there is sadness, joy.

"O Divine Master, grant that I may not so much seek to be consoled, as to console; to be understood, as to understand; to be loved, as to love; for it is in giving that we receive; it is in pardoning that we are pardoned. It is in dying that we are born to eternal life."

The room was very quiet for a long moment. When laughter from beyond the door broke the spell of his voice, and the words, Julia said, "Thank you, Troy. That was truly lovely. I'd like to send a copy to Paul, too . . . oh, dear . . . Paul!" She sat upright, pushing free of Troy's encircling arm.

He threw back his head and laughed. "Don't explain, Julia. I can guess from your face that Paul wouldn't approve of this situation."

She smoothed her hair and slipped on her shoes. "No, he wouldn't. You see, Paul and I are sort of engaged."

"Lucky Paul!" Troy put another log on the fire. "Say, how about something to eat? Mom and Lou Ellen have a buffet all arranged."

Julia shook her head.

"See here, young woman. You might decline the Judge's eggnog but my mother's creamed chicken is another matter. Family honor at stake and all that, you know."

Julia smiled agreement. While he was gone she touched her shiny nose with powder, drew on fresh lipstick, then wandered about the room, enjoying the odor of burning logs, old leather, and books. On a library table in one corner stood a tiny green spruce, rich with woodsy fragrance, strung with popcorn and cranberries, and topped by a construction-paper angel with pencil-dot eyes and a lopsided grin. She answered the angel's grin with one of her own.

Troy returned with a tray holding the creamed chicken, hot rolls, salad, pickles, steaming coffee cups. "Do you like my tree?" he asked, pulling napkin-wrapped silver from his coat pocket. "That white creation in the living room is Lou Ellen's. This one is *mine*. I made that angel in the fourth grade. Ain't it purty?"

Julia nodded her approval. "I have one like it at home but mine has paper curls and I do indeed like your tree, sir."

The food was delicious and they were hungry. Her plate

40

was almost empty when she felt Troy's eyes on her. She looked up, started to turn away, but he held her gaze.

"If that angel were a star I'd use it for wishing on. Julie Rogers, I wish you weren't 'sort of engaged' to Paul."

Julia's cheeks burned as she pushed a lone cube of chicken around the plate. Good thing it's not a star, she told herself with a sigh, because for the length of one quick heartbeat, Troy's wish was her own as well.

6

I Solemnly Pledge

January's assignment sheet moved Julia to AI West, Female Medical. Upper respiratory infections, called URI, kept the wards full and page after page of Julia's texts came alive. Anatomy had taught her the location and function of the pleura, but Mrs. Wong's hard dry cough and pain-filled eyes taught her much about pleurisy. Pneumonia, bronchitis, emphysema were no longer textbook words, symptoms, and causes, but people, patients in pain to whom nursing care meant a return to health. Julia no longer begrudged class time. Even when the class topic did not apply to one of her current patients she gave full attention because next week, next year she would need to know that the spinal nerves have two origins and that the pulmonary artery carries blood for aeration.

Rain was predicted for Friday, February 8th but by five o'clock the sky, swept clean of clouds by an ocean breeze, was as blue as a child might have colored it. The green of the hospital grounds was interrupted by wide splashes of azalea pink, rhododendron white, camellia red. But for all the freshmen noticed, San Francisco might have been caught up in a blizzard, the landscape blanketed by snow. Friday, February 8th was Capping Day!

"What time is it now, Rosie?" Julia scuffed into the room, closed the door and kicked her slippers into the closet.

"Six-ten, exactly nine minutes and twenty-seven seconds since your last time check. Between you and my mother, I may have a ventricular fibrillation yet. If she hadn't gone out for dinner I still wouldn't be dressed."

"Oh, bosh. Your mother is very nice."

"Nice, yes, but does your mother remake your bed or call you 'baby girl'?"

Julia laughed. "Well, no. But. . . ." She pulled on the blue-striped underdress and buttoned her crisp-starched apron in place. As she pulled rollers from her hair she said, "Caps—just imagine us with caps. I never thought I'd make it."

"Ha! With grades like yours? It is I who nearly foundered on the shores of Diet Therapy. It's cruelty to consider food in terms of amino acids, peristaltic waves, and a cure for scurvy."

"How you suffer," Julia scoffed. "Twenty-seven survivors out of a class of thirty-two is pretty good." She started to sit down at the dressing table, caught herself in time to prevent wrinkles in her apron. "Rosie, did you ever think Lou Ellen might not be capped?"

"Lou Ellen Archer? You're joking! She has straight A's and she's so efficient on duty she'll probably end up running the hospital."

"Maybe that's what I mean. Why didn't she go to a university for her training? Mercy concentrates on bedside nursing but at one of the university hospitals she'd be getting administrative nursing and working toward a degree as well as her R.N. I don't know—she's kind of cold with

43

the patients, you know, all business. Since you know her better than I do, I thought she might have mentioned. . . ."

"Her motives? Julia, if you don't stop analyzing people, I'm going to burn your psychology book. You're getting to be a genuine psycho-ceramic." Without waiting to be asked she explained, "A crackpot."

At 6:50 P.M. twenty-seven girls lined up in the corridor beyond the assembly room. Only the rustle of starched aprons drowned out the thud of Julia's heart. Her face was warm, her hands cold, her knees stiff with tension.

Soft organ music came through the door as it opened and closed. Mrs. Braddock went down the row passing out white tapers. She took her place at the head of the line, consulted her watch, and stage whispered, "Seven o'clock, young ladies. Are you ready?"

The blond heads and the dark, the curly and the straight nodded. For no apparent reason Mrs. Braddock frowned a bit. "Why don't we make it tomorrow night instead?" Laughter rippled along the row and dissolved the tension. Then Mrs. Braddock opened the door, and the organ music lifted.

The girls had been instructed to keep their eyes straight ahead during the processional, but in one quick sweep of the room Julia found her family in the fifth row on the right side, John and Mike half out of their chairs as they craned to see her. Without looking, Julia knew her mother and father were holding hands, for this was their moment as much as hers. She flicked them a smile and, if she'd dared, would have run to hug them.

Reaching the first row she crossed to the right as the girl before her had crossed to the left. Three steps up to the platform and she took her place in the second row of chairs.

44

Between the first tubbed palm and the speakers' podium, a table held twenty-seven very stiff white caps, caps which symbolized acceptance into and of the profession.

Eleanor Zucker, the last girl in line, took her place at the remaining vacant chair. The white-haired man at the small electric organ let his fingers pick out a soft spiritual melody.

Reverend Moresby, one of several chaplains who answered hospital calls, walked to the microphone and bowed his head for the invocation. Lois Evans made the welcome speech, senior class president Sarah Donald made the official presentation of the freshman class to the school of nursing, and Mrs. Braddock made the acceptance, concluding with "Nursing is love in action."

Julia was glad that the student speeches were short for the sake of John and wiggly Mike, but she could have listened to Mrs. Braddock much, much longer. *Nursing is love in action.* She'd have to remember those exact words to write to Paul.

"Lou Ellen Archer," the senior nurse began the roll call. The first white cap was pinned on Lou Ellen's auburn hair. Judge Archer, from his front-row seat, led the applause for his daughter as Mrs. Archer beamed. Julia's eyes followed down the row. Her brothers had come to the capping, but apparently Lou Ellen's had not.

"Sally Benson." Sally walked forward to receive her cap and the applause of the audience.

"Rosemary Dowling." Julia wished she dared clap for this new friend who had come to mean so much, but the girls on stage must remain quiet.

Name after name, cap after cap, and then her own name was called. In a moment of triumph, of humility, of Cinderella magic, Julia felt the stiff white crown of nursing settled lightly, securely on her own blonde hair.

With a queenly grace Julia returned to her chair but no queen in regal purple could match her feelings. Queens are born to their crowns, but a nursing cap must be earned.

Mrs. Braddock lit the taper on the now empty table and touched its flame to the first student's candle. From candle to candle the flame passed. The soft music ended and the hall darkened. The twenty-seven flames shone like beacons. In subdued voices the freshman class of Mercy Hospital School of Nursing in the city of San Francisco, before their friends, their parents, and their Creator, repeated together the Florence Nightingale pledge:

"I solemnly pledge myself before God, and in the presence of this assembly, to pass my life in purity, and to practice my profession faithfully. I will abstain from whatever is deleterious and mischievous and will not take or knowingly administer any harmful drug. I will do all in my power to elevate the standard of my profession and will hold in confidence all personal matters committed to my keeping, and all family affairs coming to my knowledge in the practice of my profession. With loyalty will I endeavor to aid the physician in his work and devote myself to the welfare of those committed to my care."

After a poignant moment of silence, Reverend Morseby gave the benediction, asking God's blessing and His help for each girl dedicated to the care of the sick.

Lights flashed on throughout the hall, the candles were extinguished, and from the organ came a joyous march. The end of the beginning, Julia told herself. She had, long ago, accepted nursing, and now nursing had accepted her.

The reception was nearly over. Mrs. Dowling beneath a towering rose-decked hat clung to Rosemary and exclaimed to all who would listen, "Isn't it marvelous how grown-up our girls look with uniforms and caps. Just like real nurses."

Rosemary's effort at holding a dutiful-daughter smile was almost painful to watch.

Sally Benson's father laughed and said, "They are real nurses, Mrs. Dowling, and the bedpans are real, too."

Mrs. Dowling sputtered, "I didn't mean . . . oh, for heaven sakes . . . well, who ever heard of an imitation bedpan?"

Judge Archer proposed a toast to each girl who had earned her "Dignity." He ended by saying, "May you always wear your Dignity with dignity."

Julia reached up to touch her cap, to be sure it had not evaporated or flown away.

John laughed and popped another almond crescent into his mouth. "You could always hold that thing on with thumbtacks, Sis."

Mrs. Rogers cautioned John on his manners. "By the way, where's Mike? I don't see him at the tea table. We'll have to be going soon. Oh my, it's ten-thirty already. Lights out time for you, Julia."

"Oh, no, Mom. No more lights out for me. They figure we're responsible enough by now to get the rest we need."

Mr. Rogers said, "John, see if you can round up Mike. We have a long drive home."

"I know where he is, Dad. He's talking to that old man who played the organ. Out in the hall."

Julia jumped up. "That 'old man' happens to be Dr. Clark Carey, one of the most brilliant orthopedic surgeons on the West Coast!"

"Relax, Julia," her father urged. "I imagine Dr. Carey can hold his own with Mike."

At that moment Mike came through the doorway, his small hand curled in that of the white-haired doctor. "There they are. That's my family. Julia's the one with the cap."

Julia didn't know whether to laugh or cry when Mike announced, "This is my new friend Carey."

47

"*Doctor* Carey, I'm so sorry—"

With an upraised hand the doctor cut short Julia's embarrassed apology. "I'm honored to meet the Rogers family."

As he shook hands all around, Julia searched the fine-lined face for signs of amusement but found none.

Dr. Carey turned to Mike. "Young man, I shall indeed keep an eye on your big sister and I promise to report to you from time to time."

Julia's chagrin was complete as the doctor, eyes twinkling, told her parents that Mike had stopped him in the hall and extracted his promise to watch over Julia.

As he turned to go he shook the small hand solemnly. "Michael, you'll be hearing from me."

The family goodbyes were quick warm hugs and promises to write soon. Then Julia stood alone in the living room, one arm curled around the small collection of gifts, the white nylons from her high school counselor, a framed Nightingale pledge from the family doctor, from Sue Lambert a small statue of a Dickens' character with the inscription. *Don't be a Sairey Gamp* because Sairey was the kind of nurse no nurse should be. And at the top lay an envelope from her parents containing a crisp ten dollar bill. She stood staring vacantly at the goodbyes of other parents, other classmates. Rosemary, in from seeing her mother off in a taxi, called, "Coming up now, Julia?"

Tired and a bit let down after the excitement of the evening, she started to her room. She hadn't counted on hearing from Paul but she had held a small hope.

Halfway up the stairs she heard Ma Marsh call to her from below. "Yes, Ma?"

"Did you get your flowers, Miss Rogers?"

"No, Ma. What flowers?"

She retraced her steps, followed Ma to the small ground floor kitchen. Ma opened the refrigerator and handed her a

48

florist box. "It came during capping and I almost forgot about it."

An orchid, an elegant fragile lavender orchid and a card: "Love and congratulations, Paul." Julia lifted the bloom, held it to her apron bib, cried, and then laughed. "It's lovely but I'm not going anywhere I could wear it." After a moment she said, "Would you like it, Ma? I'd be so pleased if you would."

"Thank you, Miss Rogers, but I'm afraid I'd be a bit too stylish calling girls to the phone with an orchid on my shoulder."

"Ma—may I go over to the hospital for a minute?"

"Of course, if you have a reason and judging from your face I'd say you have a reason."

The next morning a tired bedraggled woman, who two days before had attempted suicide because she thought no one cared whether she lived or died, decided life was quite worthwhile. Someone had sent her an orchid. Someone too shy to sign his name. Whoever he was he cared a lot. Such an expensive flower. So lovely, so elegant. She combed her hair and put on lipstick. You just couldn't feel unloved with an orchid on your shoulder.

Medicine comes in many containers: bottles, jugs, ampules, vials, cylinders, tubes, cartons. Occasionally it comes in a florist box. And occasionally, even when it isn't ordered by a doctor, it turns out to be "just what the doctor ordered."

49

7

Eleven to Seven, Nine Plus One

On the first day of June, Rosemary and Peggy Kellogg were assigned to Pediatrics, Lois and Lou Ellen were assigned to the Outpatient Clinic, and Julia found her name under BII Medical. Medical, again? What more could she learn on Medical? This year's coronary heart disease was like last year's coronary, this man's kidney malfunction much like any other, penicillin was penicillin whether injected into Mr. Jones's hip muscle or Mr. Smith's hip muscle. She was not disenchanted with medical nursing but she was disappointed to be doing the familiar when some of her classmates were shivering with the excitement of new challenges.

The second week of June many of the students were shivering, not from excitement but from a rapidly spreading virus. Julia's shivers, non-virus, began at 2 P.M. on Thursday in Mrs. Braddock's office.

"Ordinarily we don't give first-year students the responsibility of night duty, Miss Rogers, but this virus is playing havoc with the duty roster. I'm assigning you to eleven to seven on Ward 10 just for a night or two. The ward is small. I'm sure you won't have any trouble. Now, you run along

50

to bed. Ward 10 has mostly chronic cases, not really busy enough to keep you awake, so you get some sleep."

Sleep? Certainly. Every student claimed an accumulated weariness that would allow her to sleep standing up, if ever she had an uninterrupted five minutes. Sleep in the afternoon? An unheard of luxury. Clean pajamas, good mattress, quiet room. Ah! But wooed and wanted, sleep would not come. Julia could no more sleep when ordered than sneeze when ordered.

At five she gave up and went to supper. At six she tried again, every muscle, tendon, nerve willing; but her busy brain percolated like a coffeepot on high heat. Seven, eight, nine—endless wide-eyed hours. At nine-thirty she was drowsy. Too late. A cool shower brought her awake. The last thing she put in her uniform pocket was the plastic-encased card with the Prayer of St. Francis, Troy's gift delivered by Lou Ellen one rainy March afternoon. No message, but none was needed. Tonight Julia added a line of her own: Oh, Lord, help me stay awake. Eyelids drooping, she headed for the hospital.

Ward 10, once a sundeck, was converted to a ward during a long ago war. It was used primarily for the chronically ill, and the atmosphere was as much old ladies' home as hospital.

Waiting at the desk, Julia watched the gleam of a flashlight move from bed to bed. The three to eleven nurse finished her rounds and walked to the desk.

"Last-minute check and everyone's settled so you should have an easy night, Rogers." The junior nurse flipped the patient cardex and gave the report. Nine patients, one empty bed, no red markers to indicate critically ill cases. Almost nothing to do until 6 A.M. medications and morning care.

Together they counted the sedatives and small supply of narcotics. Each signed the tally sheet indicating the count

51

correct. The older student locked the case and surrendered the key. From that moment the safety of the narcotic and sedative supply on Ward 10 rested with Julia.

"The night supervisor, Miss Powell, will be around shortly. Be sure to get her permission before giving a sedative or a narcotic. Sometimes Mrs. Fox in Bed 1 wakes up and wants a cup of tea. When you take her the tea, make some excuse to leave or she'll talk your leg off and wake up half the ward. All set now?"

Julia nodded.

"Oh, there's my medical nursing text. I marked the pages that match our little old ladies just in case you want to be more familiar with their cases. You'll like Miss Powell, stern, kind—the sort you need when you *really* need someone." She yawned and picked up her knitting bag. "Mrs. Wimple, Bed 2, is teaching me to make argyles. Oh, look at the time. I'll miss dinner if I doodle around here any longer. What's on the menu?"

Julia smiled. "Chef's Delight. Isn't that a nice way of saying leftovers?"

Flashlight in hand Julia walked into the ward, her rubber-soled footsteps loud in the sleeping stillness. She cupped one hand over the beacon of light and checked each patient. The nine women slept undisturbed and Julia returned to the desk to begin the long, lonely watch.

At eleven-thirty a tall, heavy-set woman about fifty approached the desk. Her bearing was almost as stiffly starched as her white uniform. Julia stood up and said, "Good evening, Miss Powell."

"Good evening, Miss Rogers. How are your patients?"

She listened carefully as Julia reported her charges. Miss Powell knew each case history, each diagnosis as though this small ward were her only concern.

52

"One empty bed. Let's hope it stays empty." Miss Powell looked intently at Julia. "What's wrong, Miss Rogers? You seem nervous."

Julia fidgeted with her bandage scissors. "I'm just plain scared, I guess, being here alone with the patients."

Miss Powell's face sobered. "You are never given such responsibility until you are prepared for it, Miss Rogers. Mrs. Braddock is a far better judge of your ability than you are, and the welfare of the patients is her first concern. Do you think she would entrust them to you if she doubted your capability?"

Julia stood mute as the rebuke stung her ears.

"And you are not alone. The telephone, there on the chart desk, will bring you help anytime you need it. You are never alone when you are part of a hospital team."

The telephone jangled. Miss Powell answered. A voice loud with urgency leaped through the earpiece. "Room two-one-seven? I'll be there immediately."

Julia watched, open-mouthed, the most dignified flight of feet she'd ever seen.

When the clock indicated the end of the first hour, she drew midnight lines on each chart to show the start of a new hospital day. She filled out requisitions for stock drugs and bandage supplies and checked each patient's medical supply. She read the textbook for a while, hoping Mrs. Fox would call for tea. If she woke the whole ward there'd be plenty to do. When her eyes burned for sleep, Julia splashed ice water in her face and made rounds for the umpteenth time. The empty bed looked inviting and Julia viewed each sleeping patient with envy. She walked to the far end of the ward and stood at the open window. The old trees, their lace of leaves drooping from gnarled branches, swayed a lullaby rhythm in the night breeze.

A sound at the desk cleared any thought of sleep from her mind. She hurried through the ward and looked about anxiously. A senior stuck her head out from the tiny linen closet and said, "Hi! I was just looking to see if you have a light cradle. You're getting a patient. There's a woman down in Emergency with an infected foot. Oh, I'm here to relieve you for coffee break. I'm Miss Russell, night float."

"Float?"

"Yes. I'm not assigned to any special floor, just help out wherever I'm needed and relieve for coffee breaks when I have a chance."

"I'll hurry," Julia promised.

"Take your time, Rogers. Have two cups. You'll need it. Just wait until you try to settle the ward after a 2 A.M. admission."

Julia hurried to the dining room, downed a quick cup of coffee and hurried back.

The ward was fully lighted and the curtains drawn around Bed 6. Miss Russell was helping the patient from wheel chair to bed. The float nurse adjusted an awkward light cradle over the woman's acutely inflamed foot, then swung sheet and blankets over the cradle and smoothed them with a practiced economy of motions.

She turned and said, "Miss Rogers, this is your new patient, Mrs. Macadoo."

Julia flashed an amiable smile and the small dark-eyed woman responded with a courteous nod.

"Excuse us for a minute, Mrs. Macadoo," Miss Russell said. Julia pushed the empty wheel chair as they walked to the desk.

"Her admission sheet and orders are there on the desk. I'll get the solution and equipment from supply for the foot soaks. The drug clerk will be up with the penicillin shortly.

54

She's Dr. Moody's patient but the resident on call, Dr. Graham, admitted her and wrote orders. I'll be back to help you as soon as I finish coffee breaks." Miss Russell left.

Julia glanced at the admission sheet, then paused to read the orders with care.

The neon blaze still lighted the ward and the patients shifted restlessly. Julia stopped first at Mrs. Macadoo, gave her a cool drink of water and turned her bed light on dim. She moved from bed to bed, turning pillows, smoothing sleep-wrinkled sheets. She turned out the ceiling lights and returned to the alcove that housed the medical supplies. The penicillin had been delivered. Julia read its label, checked Dr. Graham's order and prepared the dosage.

"Mrs. Macadoo, the doctor ordered this injection for you. Are you allergic to any of the antibiotics?"

"Isn't that funny? The doctor asked the same thing. Like I told him, I don't know because I never had cause to take 'em. I've got cause enough now, the way my foot pains."

With an alcohol sponge, Julia cleansed the deep-muscled area of the patient's right hip. She injected the needle into the spot that cleared the sciatic nerve and large blood vessels and administered the dosage slowly. "I'll be back in a jiffy with the soaks for your foot. Here's your signal cord. Just push this button if you want me."

At the desk Julia found the chart headings completed and a note with the new patient's temperature, pulse, respiration, blood pressure, and weight, thanks to Miss Russell's kindness. Julia looked again at the blood pressure. It was unusually high and no doubt accounted for the early morning admission for an infection that might otherwise have been handled by the outpatient clinic.

In the utility room she heated the solution for the soaks and prepared a tray with all the equipment needed for the

55

treatment. The buzz of a patient's signal called her to the ward.

Mrs. Macadoo was sitting up, gasping for breath. Her attempt to talk was thick-tongued and unintelligible. Julia rolled up the head of the bed to give her support and turned the bedlight up bright.

Edema of the larynx. Swelling of the tongue and throat. The words from her medical nursing text registered clearly in her mind. She ran to the phone, listened for the click of the operator's plug-in. "Severe reaction to penicillin. Swelling of the larynx. Get Miss Powell quickly!"

With a hurried scoop into the ice chest, Julia filled a glass and grabbed a spoon with the other hand. She must think of some way to calm her. Panic could be fatal now. As she neared the bed she forced her steps to a slower pace. "Mrs. Macadoo," she pronounced each syllable in a slow deliberate manner. "Lean back a little and hold your mouth open. I have some ice chips here." She spooned a small amount into the open mouth. "This will help control the swelling until the doctor gets here."

The wild fear in Mrs. Macadoo's face eased slightly.

All at once the ward was full of the hospital team. Miss Powell, Dr. Graham, Miss Russell, followed shortly by an O.R. nurse with a cloth-wrapped tray in her arms.

Dr. Graham gave a hushed command, "Adrenalin, eight minums, immediately."

Julia hurried to the medicine area. Miss Russell followed, grabbed the sphygmomanometer and blood pressure cuff and returned to the ward.

Julia reached for the glass ampule of adrenalin and silently thanked God that the "everything in its place" rule was strictly enforced. With sterile forceps she picked up the hypodermic syringe, adjusted the needle in place and laid it on a sterile gauze sponge. She read the label on the glass

56

ampule, used a tiny saw-edged file to make a break line and snapped off the top. Heart pounding, she slipped the needle into the open end of the ampule and pulled the plunger back to fill the syringe with the ordered amount. She held the small vial with a steady hand to reread the label, then raced to the doctor's side.

"Adrenalin, eight minums, Dr. Graham. Will you give it intravenously?"

The doctor eyed the gauge attached to the blood pressure cuff and said, "No, I'm concerned about her pressure. Make it five minums, subcutaneously."

"Adrenalin, five minums." Julia repeated the order as she swabbed the patient's upper arm and injected the medication.

The doctor waited a few moments and when the gasping remained unrelieved, he nodded to the surgical nurse. "We can't risk more adrenalin with her pressure. Set up for a tracheotomy."

Miss Powell reappeared with an orderly who carried a heavy surgical lamp.

Miss Russell rolled the bed down and placed a sand bag under the patient's shoulders to stretch the neck and make the trachea more prominent.

The operating room nurse folded back the tray cover, slipped on sterile gloves, lined up the assortment of gleaming instruments. The surgical light flooded the area with blue-white brightness. Mrs. Macadoo seized Julia's hand in a viselike grip. Julia, her heart pounding in her ears, gulped air as if she would breathe for both.

Dr. Graham swabbed the patient's neck with an alcohol sponge and his gloved fingers felt for the exact area for the incision. With a scalpel he made a tiny slit in the indented area, two fingers width below the adam's apple, and slipped a tiny silver tube into the opening. Through this small

57

incision, below the level of the swelling, a rush of air entered to feed oxygen-starved lungs. The nurses and doctor heaved a unanimous sigh as the first easy breath sped home to assure life, where seconds before, death seemed inevitable. Mrs. Macadoo released her grip and Julia felt a hot tingle in her fingers.

The doctor took a single stitch at either end of the incision tube and, seizing the cords which dangled from the flange of the tube, tied them about Mrs. Macadoo's neck. "This will keep it from sliding out or being coughed out," the young doctor explained. "We'll let you rest a bit before we get down to the business of reducing the swelling. Miss Powell, will you arrange her transfer to the intensive care ward?"

The supervisor nodded approval, then walked with Julia to the desk. "I'm pleased that Mrs. Braddock's appraisal was completely justified. You did very well, Miss Rogers."

Julia thrilled at this high praise, but a sweep of humility reminded her that she was but a small part of this life-saving team.

A bit later, with the patients settled for a few more hours of sleep, and the tracheotomy tube under Miss Russell's capable eye while the transfer was being arranged, Julia sat down. Mrs. Macadoo's chart lay on the desk open to the lined page entitled "Nurses Notes." According to this bare sheet, the woman hadn't even been admitted. Julia squeezed the red-inked pen and printed:

"White female, age 52, admitted to Ward 10, Bed 6. Admitting diagnosis: inflammation, right foot. T.101.8 P. 92 R. 20. B.P. 195/115." That much was easy, routine. "Light cradle over right foot, as ordered." Julia hesitated. How to record in the tiny space here the disciplined excitement, the life or death drama which had just unfolded? The emotion of the battle remained untold as tight words recorded: penicillin, reaction, adrenalin, tracheotomy, relief.

As she stood to take the chart to Miss Russell, Julia's attention was caught by the medical nursing text on the desk. She almost laughed aloud at a question she'd asked herself days earlier: What more could she learn on Medical? The answer now was easy. The more you know the more you know there is to know.

8

Warm Forceps

August second began for Julia at 5:50 A.M. She couldn't wait an instant longer. "Rosie." She aimed her toe to nudge the sleeping huddle in the other bed. "Rosemary." No answer. "Rosemary Dowling!"

"Wha-what? What time is it?"

"Time to say hello to me—that's what time it is. Didn't you even miss me?"

"I missed you." Rosemary rolled over and burrowed her head beneath the pillow.

"I'm gone three weeks and—"

Rosemary lifted the pillow. "And you didn't write once! Now you're itching to know if Peggy really got married and if Lou Ellen is actually assigned to Surgery and where we go to get our junior stripes. My answer is 'no comment.'"

Julia zipped back the cover and tossed her pillow at the once-again inert form on the next bed. The well-aimed counterfire caught Julia off balance, tumbling her to the floor. "I'll write. Next vacation I'll write."

"Okay." Rosemary sat up yawning, reached for her hair-brush, yawned again. "Peggy quit to marry Jack what's-his-name—the engineering student she met at Archer's open house. They're off to Peru or somewhere, wherever his job is."

"Gee, that's too bad. Peggy had all the makings of a fine nurse."

Rosemary frowned. "She had a hard time deciding. I should have such a choice."

"You wouldn't quit!"

"No, I wouldn't. Anyway, Lou Ellen's lost her room mate and. . . ." Rosemary brushed her hair vigorously.

Julia drew a long deep breath. "And she asked you to room with her when we move downstairs next week."

Rosemary nodded without looking around. "What do you think?" Their eyes met in the dressing table mirror . . . serious for a moment, then Julia's crinkled with laughter. "I think she's a nut. Has she seen you by dawn's early light? Does she know you snore?"

Rosemary dimpled. "Thanks, Julia. I don't want to change either but this sudden popularity does wonders for a gal's morale. I guess this has been the best summer of my whole life. Pediatrics and a week at the Archer's cabin on the Russian River and day after tomorrow we get our junior stripes." The buzz of the alarm clock just then brought a laugh from both girls. "I just hope this crack-of-dawn arising doesn't set a precedent," Rosemary said, picking up her towel and heading for the shower.

Over the steamy hiss of the showers Rosemary called to Julia in the next cubicle, "So how was your vacation?"

"Nice. Paul was home the first week. He's off to Okinawa, you know, for a whole year."

"What happened to electronics school?"

"He didn't qualify."

"Too bad."

"After he left we spent a week camping at Yosemite. Betsy

61

and Phil were home for a few days too. They're expecting in December. All in all I had a mighty fine vacation."

"What about Troy?" Both showers turned off at once and there was a long moment of silence.

From the other side of the room came the swishing sound of a toothbrush and, "Yes, what about old tall and ugly?"

"Oh, hi, Lou Ellen," Julia called, glad that she had announced her presence. "Troy stopped by one day last week . . . to say hello." Julia was glad, too, for the cubicle walls. Her face might be saying more than her voice.

"And?" pressed Rosemary.

"That's all." Lazily toweling off, Julia thought back to that strangely unsettling day. Troy had dropped by as casually as a neighbor might. He had taken her and her mother to lunch, Mike and her out to the lake for a swim, accepted Mrs. Rogers' invitation to stay for barbecued chicken at six and strawberry shortcake in late evening. Casual as you please. Like an old family friend. Stopped by to say hello and to tell about his six weeks in Mexico helping a student group dig a village well. Hello, Julie. But he seemed to be visiting her whole family.

As she clipped her cap in place Rosemary said, "Come on, my moon-eyed roommate. It's twenty-five to seven. We'll miss breakfast if we don't move the metacarpals."

"Metatarsals, Rosie," Julia gently corrected. "Metacarpals are finger bones."

"So walk on your hands, but let's go."

They were half way to the hospital when Rosemary let out a shriek. "Julia Rogers, do you know what you've done! You've gotten me up, and gotten me dressed, and ruined my whole day. I'm on three to eleven!"

They moved to the second floor the following week. Julia grinned everytime she thought of Rosemary's comment on

62

the new room color. "I must be more nurse than I thought. This paint reminds me of bile."

Julia wore her narrow black stripe with great pride and viewed the new class of probationers with pity and concern. "Surely we didn't look that greenhorn, when we came," she confided to Rosemary. But she felt like a probationer all over again when, two days later, she knocked at the door marked Hospital Engineer.

This part of the basement, beyond the dining room and supply center, was strange. Her knowledge of the furnace room, which also housed the big gas-jet incinerator, was meager. There must be such a place because steam hissed through the radiators at the turn of a handle and the whoosh of paper-wrapped refuse, when dropped through the little wall door in each floor's utility room, indicated it was going somewhere to be destroyed. But only this morning, when the whoosh took a surgical instrument along with Mrs. McGarrity's soiled dressing, was Julia forced to find the bottom of the refuse drop. The floor supervisor had been unnerving. There had been no reprimand for careless handling of the forceps, no look of disdain, only quiet patience as she explained where to find Uncle Jerry.

Another hospital relative, Julia mused. First Ma Marsh who really mothers, but why Uncle for a man who tends the heat? Would you also call the cleaning woman Auntie Septic?

A second rap on the door brought an answer. Uncle Jerry, short, fat-faced, gray-thatched, and looking as old as the hospital itself, smiled a welcome.

"Sorry to keep you waiting, Miss. I was on the phone. Surgery wants more steam to run the autoclave. They're rushed for sterile supplies this morning. Don't usually autoclave the surgery packs until afternoon." He explained all this as though she knew it and he was just making conversation. "Excuse me while I send up some steam." He scarcely looked as he whirled a round handle, one among a maze of handles and gauges. Then giving one gauge a satisfied nod, he turned to Julia.

The idea that the arch-efficiency of the tiled and stainless steel operating room depended to some small degree on this odd little man startled her.

"What can I do for you, Miss? Did you lose something down the incinerator shaft?"

Julia was taken aback. How did he know? "Yes, Mister . . ."

"Just Uncle Jerry, Miss. My last name is important only to the bookkeeper. Even Mrs. Braddock calls me Uncle Jerry." His voice held unreserved pride.

"Do you know Mrs. Braddock?" She was embarrassed by the foolish, too-quick question. "But of course you do."

"Oh, I knew Jeannie Braddock when she was a little girl. Jeannie Hansen she was then. Watched her grow up and go through training here and on to get her degree and such. Fine woman! Fine woman! Makes fine fruitcake too." He wagged his chin in approval. "Now, what did you say you lost?"

"Forceps, about this long." Julia measured six inches with her fingers.

The old man turned another handle, this one below a wide metal door. As he picked up a short-handled rake, a chuckle shook his well-rounded middle. "You girls come down, looking all serious, like you were the only one who ever dropped the wrong thing down the shaft. Sooner or later I meet every student at Mercy. Been meeting them here for thirty-five years, right by this door. I guess I know more nurses than anyone else in town unless it's Mrs. Stengall over in the laundry. She meets them all, looking for something they lost in the dirty linen. And until you come looking, you never know that it takes more than patients and nurses to make a hospital. Not that I'm blaming you, understand. I guess we all see Mercy in our own way. Me, by how many pounds of steam, Mrs. Stengall by how many sheets and towels, the kitchen people by how many diet trays and dirty dishes. But it takes all of us to make Mercy go, each giving the best way he can."

Julia warmed to the talkative Uncle Jerry. "You find us out, eh, all our secret slip-ups?"

He swung open the metal door, stepped back to avoid a blast of heat from the cooling jets. "No, Miss, not *all* your secrets. Just the ones that bring you down here."

Her glance fell on the workworn fingers which emphasized his words. Age, heat, and thirty-five years of service to Mercy had given the hands a leathery roughness, yet somehow they appeared gentle for all their strength.

He reached the rake into the ashes, dragged it slowly until he heard the clink of metal meeting metal, then pulled it to the opening. A spill of waste lay before the rake tines. And there they were, those elusive forceps, blacked-and-blued by the fire.

Julia looked again. "No, that's the wrong pair. That's a curved Kelly. I dropped a straight one."

"Guess we'll have company then. Someone'll be down for these." He repeated the rake drag and brought the right forceps to the front.

A nervous tap sounded at the furnace room door. Julia was surprised when she turned to find Lou Ellen there, her mantle of assurance and calm poise conspicuously absent.

As their eyes met, Lou Ellen stiffened and shifted her gaze. In a cool tone she said, "Did you find a curved Kelly in the incinerator, sir? One seems to be missing from the O.R. I'm new there so, naturally, I'm the one to come looking."

Uncle Jerry gave her a crinkle-eyed smile. "Yes, Miss Archer, here's your instrument. I've been hoping to meet you again. Your father and I trade iris tubers occasionally. The last time I saw you was in your garden, when you were about twelve. Come in and talk, if you have a minute."

Lou Ellen obeyed the command that sounded like an invitation.

Julia, feeling she had been dismissed, picked up the grimy, still warm forceps and left. Somehow meeting Lou Ellen in the heater room gave her an exquisite satisfaction. Her mother would call this cream-on-whiskers smile most unbecoming but for one long moment Julia let herself enjoy the situation.

Once in a while even a nurse with a junior stripe acts nine instead of nineteen.

9

A Scrub and a Flub

SURGERY:
M. Scott
G. Develin
R. Howard
L. Thorton
L. Archer
J. Rogers

Unbelieving Julia stared at the roster. Surgery: J. Rogers. Quick as a blink she spun through time and space to a surgical amphitheater where students watched in rapt silence. J. Rogers, masked and gowned, serves instruments to a handsome young brain surgeon. While he stitches in the final sutures Dr. Cerebellum announces, "We've done it again, Miss Rogers. We've saved another life." A sigh that is like applause rises from the observers. As the patient is wheeled away to the recovery room another surgeon approaches. "Miss Rogers, I'm ready to do a heart valve repair. Will you be my surgical nurse?" She is tired but she cannot refuse. "Of course, Dr. Cardiac, but we'll have to hurry. Dr. Bonegraft is waiting for my help and you know how impatient he is." Dr. Cardiac chortles, "For you, Miss Rogers, he'll wait."

At seven-ten, Julia hung her uniform in the dressing-room, pulled the shapeless green dress over her head, and began a ten-thumbed struggle with a gauze triangle that was to cover her hair.

A seven weeks' veteran of the O.R., Lou Ellen converted her triangle into a trim turban with three deft hand-over-hand motions. She moved with important steps to the chalk board that showed the day's schedule of operations and read aloud, "Exploratory laparotomy at 8:00, Room Two, followed by a thyroidectomy at 10:00. Looks like I'll be busy. Rogers, you have a T&A at 8:00, another at 9:00, and an ingrown toenail at 10:00. Come on, I'll show you where to scrub."

Julia, with a helping hand from a graduate, anchored the turban with a hopeful knot, grabbed a gauze mask, and followed the soft swish of Lou Ellen's scrub dress to a room lined with deep sinks. Julia reminded herself that she knew how to do all the things she must do this morning. Hadn't the ward instructor gone over every step of scrubbing, gowning, and working in a sterile field? She had even practiced each procedure in the classroom. But, here, where it counted, her mind was suddenly a total blank. Imitating Lou Ellen's motions, she reached for a sterile scrub brush, and slid her knee into a U-shaped handle. A slight swing of her knee sent a fine spray of water from the shower head over the sink and wet the brush. The tap of a button on the floor shot liquid green soap from a tiny spout near the water spray.

"Start with your nails, Rogers. No, look at the clock first. Time yourself for ten minutes, five on either hand. Now, nails first, fingers, palms, backs of hands, wrists, forearms, then right up to the elbow. Keep your hands up, so the water flows away from the area you've scrubbed. Once you've completed the fingers, don't touch them again except with clean water . . . same thing right up the arm. That's it but scrub harder, in a circular motion." Lou Ellen kept a constant eye on Julia's flying brush and jerky water spray. By the fifth knee swing, Julia mastered a smooth glide of water on, water off.

Satisfied that the scrubbing was progressing properly, Lou Ellen began a rundown on what to, where to, and how to in the operating room. "Your T&A instrument tray is set up by the circulating nurse. Once you're scrubbed, you touch nothing that isn't sterile, the instruments are simple and you have almost nothing to do, except to stay out of the doctor's way. Scrubbing for a tonsillectomy is just to break you in. In a few days, you'll be scrubbing for more difficult minor surgery. You'll really have the feel of things and know your instruments, too, before you scrub for majors. What's Miss Powell's phrase for night duty jitters? Oh, yes! 'You are never sent until you are prepared!' Well, that applies here, too."

Julia, scrubbing until her fingers ached and her skin smarted, listened in awed silence to Lou Ellen's rapid-fire enlightenment. She wondered, briefly, how Lou Ellen knew Miss Powell's pet phrase, but discretion prevented inquiry.

Scrubs completed, Lou Ellen dipped her arms, elbow deep, into a container of alcohol solution and backed through the swinging door which led to Room Two. Julia dipped her arms too and winced at the cold, stinging liquid. Her arms dripped dry as she walked, hands high and knees wobbly, to the smaller operating room which was to be her air-conditioned trial by fire.

A graduate greeted her with a sterile towel, held by forceps. Julia dried her hands, slipped into a green (open down the back) sterile gown and eased on sterile rubber gloves. The circulating nurse adjusted a gauze mask over her nose and mouth, then tied the back of the shoe-length operating gown. A whir of wheels announced the arrival of the patient.

A freckle-spattered nose and crew cut on little Mr. Tonsils caused Julia to do a double take. He looked just like Mike, all but the wide brown eyes which were searching the room.

"Where's the bottles?" he inquired.

Julia, puzzled, asked, "What bottles, fella?"

"The ones you keep the tonsils in. George, he's my friend, well, George had his tonsils out and he said you keep 'em all in bottles. I want to see George's bottle."

Lanky, broad-shouldered Dr. Johnson, in green scrub clothes that looked like short-sleeved pajamas, ambled into the room to answer, "Oh, the bottles are . . . well, we'll see about the bottles later. Right now we're going to show you a funny kind of mask, kind of like a tea strainer, only all wrapped up in gauze." As he talked he donned mask and gown. "See, I have a mask over my nose. Now let's see how this one fits over your nose. When you smell something funny, just blow it away."

Drops of ether fell in a steady rhythm and the youngster obligingly blew into the mask, breathed deeply of the anesthetic, and blew away again. His resonant snore indicated all was ready. That is, all but Julia.

In an unconscious effort to help the boy, she too had inhaled deeply, breathing in enough of the ether to make her dizzy. Busy with the task at hand, the doctor was not aware of Julia's plight until she moaned, "I think I'm going to faint."

Without turning his head, he ordered, "Move back, then, away from the Mayo table. I don't want the instruments contaminated."

Julia shuffled back a step and the circulating nurse spoke sharply, "Oh, no you don't, Miss Rogers. We don't have time for you to faint this morning."

70

And Julia didn't.

The morning hours moved swiftly along. One scrub over, another begun. Stretchers purring over tiled floors. Instruments gleaming importantly under the giant shadowless lights. Gloved fingers performing their sleight-of-hand magic as the procession of the pained were given a new pain, a healing pain that, days later, would be only itches from stitches and let-me-tell-you-about-my-operation conversation.

After her last scrub, Julia edged into a corner of Room Two where another student served instruments, always the right instrument, into the surgeon's never-kept-waiting hand.

"Sponge count?" he asked of the second scrubbed student.

"Sponge count correct, doctor," Lou Ellen reported.

Incision closed with fine black sutures, specimen labeled and sent to the lab, dressing in place, patient to recovery room. "Hold her chin up, keep the airway open." Instruments through a green soap bath and into the sterilizer. Time for lunch.

Lecture from one to two. A heat-lazy fly toyed with the instructor's ear and Julia's thoughts wandered from the pediatrics lecture to a pediatric patient, small and freckled, who thought tonsils were bottled and saved. A smile betrayed her errant thoughts and her face flushed hot when the doctor-lecturer asked, "Are you with us, Miss Rogers?"

After class, Julia rushed to catch up with Lou Ellen. "What do we do now? There isn't any afternoon surgery, is there?"

"Not usually," Lou Ellen answered pleasantly. "Unless it's an emergency. We oil instruments, make up the packs for tomorrow's schedule, and autoclave supplies. You're to be freshman nurse on my scrub team, but we're not on call until tomorrow. The other team is on tonight. How did you make out this morning?"

Julia grinned and told her about little Mr. Tonsils, carefully omitting the near-fainting episode. Lou Ellen's friendly

71

attitude might change if anything so inept as a first-scrub faint were mentioned and Julia longed for her professional approval.

"I was wondering, Lou Ellen, if we could get some . . . something in a bottle to satisfy the little fellow's curiosity?"

Lou Ellen reflected a moment. "Sure! You go on up to the O.R. I'm going to stop by the dining room."

Julia was puzzled but asked no questions. She proceeded to the surgery workroom and explained Lou Ellen's delay.

Some twenty minutes later, Lou Ellen stood in the work-room doorway and announced brightly, "Here we are, two peeled grapes in a bottle of water. Think they'll pass as tonsils?"

The girls at the work table smiled and nodded approval as they oiled kellys, hemastats, retractors, and a myriad of other instruments used in the day's scrubs. No one complained that Lou Ellen had been playing while all others worked. Little Mr. Tonsils had caught the imagination of all, and they were delighted to be in on the fun.

"There you are, Rogers. Your little friend should be satisfied with these."

"Oh, gosh," Julia stammered. "I don't want to do it alone. Will you go with me, Lou Ellen, when we're through making up the packs and autoclaving?"

Lou Ellen declined, then, after a moment said, "All right, Rogers. I'll watch your little show." Her tone returned to cool efficiency. "I have to drop some surgical report sheets off there, anyway."

Later, on their way to the Pediatric Wing, Lou Ellen explained, "I feel I owe you something for not telling anyone about my instrument down the incinerators slip-up. I thought sure you'd jump at the chance, after all the times I've ribbed you."

Julia's cheeks colored as she remembered what a temptation it had been to discredit the Lou Ellen-can-do-no-wrong theory. "Forget it, gal. When I'm half the nurse you are, I might feel I have the right to ridicule."

"Half the nurse!" Lou Ellen stopped and looked squarely at Julia. "Why, I'm no nurse at all. I'm fine on theory, efficient when the patient is under anesthesia or unconscious, but bedside nursing, where you have to feel for the patient —I'm just zero there. I've tried. I've watched patients warm to you, and I've tried to sense their needs, but I just can't." A sigh spoke her feelings, even more clearly than words.

"But you thought of the fake tonsils," Julia protested. "You felt for that little boy when you heard how Dr. Johnson put him off."

Lou Ellen scoffed. "Oh, anyone is a pushover for a child. I don't mean that. I mean the moanin', groanin' adults, the people who require more than a sedative and a back rub. I just don't get through to them."

Julia searched for the right thing to say. Failing, she held up the bottle, saying, "Let's find our boy."

As they approached his bed, he lay dozing, curled in the covers like a young animal in a nest. He opened one eye and peered up at them. "Who're you?"

"We're the surgery nurses," Julia answered. "You wanted to see your tonsils, so here they are."

The brown eyes stared in disbelief. "Dr. Johnson was here and said the lab doctor cut 'em up to see if they had germs in 'em. How'd you get 'em whole again?"

Julia, chagrined by her misjudgment of Dr. Johnson and at being trapped by her own scheme, was unable to answer.

Lou Ellen came to the rescue. "Well, what do you know, Miss Rogers? We picked up the wrong tonsils."

The boy suggested hopefully, "Maybe those are George's. Let's see 'em."

Julia added weakly, "Yes, these must be George's."

73

10

Double Heartbeat

As she pushed through the white double doors, Julia looked down the dimly lit corridor. You're a fickle woman, Miss Rogers. For three months Surgery was everything, and now here you are liking Maternity just as much. Six months ago your greatest concern was the life of the burn patient in 202 and now you can't even remember his name. Three weeks ago your whole world came wrapped in a receiving blanket, and when the tiny fingers of the newborn clutched at your heart, you felt you'd be content to be a nursery nurse forever. Now someone else lullabies the babies because you are involved with the labor patients. Was it wrong to forget the yesterdays and give her attention and affection to this moment's need? Right or wrong, tonight she was assigned to General Maternity and there would be no time to ponder such a big question. What was there about night duty that prompted deep thoughts and searching questions?

The hour before midnight dragged by, most of the patients slept soundly, and the one labor patient was under the watchful eye of the charge nurse, Mrs. Watts. When the midnight lines on the charts were finished and the other student had gone for coffee, Julia pulled two letters from her apron pocket, one from Paul who wrote almost daily from Okinawa and one from Betsy Matthews Smith. Phil's construction job in Eureka was almost finished and the next contract was to be in San Francisco. Julia smiled. How good it would be to see Betsy again. She had grown apart from most of her high school friends. As she had explained to her mother, they talked mostly of clothes and how could she join in when eighty percent of her wardrobe was uniforms? The girls had been curious about her hospital experiences but she could not break her pledge to keep in confidence the affairs of her patients. Betsy would be different. Betsy would. . . .

The telephone rang, returning Julia to maternity and night duty.

"This is admitting. Customer coming up."

Julia went to tell Mrs. Watts, then walked down the corridor, picturing herself the gracious friendly nurse, on hand to welcome, to reassure. The last time she'd tried this the woman, in for her ninth delivery, called Julia "that nice freckled-nosed child." But if the new patient were young and frightened even a freckle-nosed nurse was reassuring.

The door flipped back and Julia stared, frozen, wide-mouthed, her posture of a confident nurse dissolved. "Betsy! Phil! What are you doing here?"

Phil stammered, "We're . . . she's . . . you know . . . a baby. We're here to have the baby."

Betsy threw her arms about Julia and their laughter and tears mingled. Julia recovered composure first as the nurse in her took command. With one arm supporting Betsy, she led the way to Labor Room Two. After asking Phil to wait in the Father's Room Julia helped Betsy into a hospital gown and bed. During the admission routine Betsy told of arriving in San Francisco the day before and of what a temptation it had been to go home to her mother in San

75

Dorcas. "I was determined to stay with Phil, but tonight . . . oh, Julia you don't know how glad I was to see you!"

"Any nurse would do what I'll do, Betsy. Of course a familiar face is a nice bonus, but you'll be fine. It's the mama's girls that cause themselves trouble." For all Betsy's maturity she still seemed frightened, tense. Julia gave her the ordered sedative, then from her classroom knowledge, outlined the steps of a normal delivery, telling her what to expect and how to assist. Panic faded from Betsy's eyes and gradually she relaxed.

When the doctor and Mrs. Watts came in to check Betsy's progress, Julia went to call Phil. He was as tense as Betsy had been at first. Once more Julia gave an explanation of the normal steps of birth. And once more she marveled at the effect. Simple facts, simply stated turned Phil's fear into a healthy concern, concern that Betsy would correctly understand as a sign of his love. Nursing was more than physical care. Julia had long known this. But tonight she found one more dimension.

Now feet were flying. The patient in Room One must be wheeled to Delivery. Doctor, anesthetist, scrub nurse in quick procession. Mrs. Watts issued orders on the run. Julia winged from one task to another. Telephone jangling. Another admission. Hurry. Hurry.

Check on Mrs. Smith.

"Keep up the good work, Betsy, and you'll have your son in another hour."

"You mean daughter," protested Phil.

"Son," insisted Betsy.

"Whoa, you two," laughed Julia. "Let time settle this argument."

Time did. One hour and twenty minutes later, Julia finished the last notation for Betsy's chart.

5:10 Dr. Duval scrubbed.

5:13 Nitrous oxide anesthesia administered.

5:17 Normal male infant delivered.

5:20 Silver nitrate sol. to baby's eyes.

5:21 Identification bracelet secured to infant's rt. arm; footprint taken.

5:26 Respiration and color of infant satisfactory.

5:30 Infant to nursery.

Coming out through the doors marked "Delivery Rooms: No Admittance," Julia pulled the gauze mask from her nose. Phil was slumped on a hard bench, fatigue-smudged circles beneath his eyes, his hands knotted together, the picture of all worried waiting fathers. Julia felt anew the sweep of warmth she experienced that first day on Maternity when her stethoscope found the tiny heartbeat inches from the sustaining mother heartbeat.

"Phil."

His eyes leaped up, found her smile. He bounded to his feet. "Yes? Yes?"

"Betsy is fine, and you have a beautiful baby boy."

"Are you sure? Betsy's okay. And he's a boy? Are you positive?"

"I am positively positive."

Phil grabbed her by the shoulders and twirled her around. "Oh, thank you, Julia. Thank you. Thank you. Thank you!"

Julia pulled free, caught her cap as it tumbled, and tried to quiet him. "Phil Smith, you're going to wake up the entire hospital."

"Good. Let's wake everybody! So they can know about my son. I'm a father and Betsy's a mother and we have a son! We're going to name him Paul."

"Paul?" She bit her tongue to keep from adding "You can't. That name is mine, ours."

"Yes, Paul. For Betsy's father. Paul Matthews Smith. Too bad it's not a girl. We could have named her for you, Julia. We'll let you be Aunt Julia, okay?"

"That's fine, Phil. Just fine." But for a moment Julia felt like an aging spinster watching as life and love passed by. She smiled, more at her foolishness than at Phil. "If you're reasonably calm now, the nursery nurse will show you your handsome young son. Just beyond the desk. That big window."

Lights flashed in the hall and Julia knew she was needed. How strange, here in the middle of a bustling life-filled world she felt lonely. Very lonely. Paul. A tiny Paul and a faraway Paul. Aunt Julia, nearly twenty and not a ring on her fingers.

11

A Special Gift

Julia pulled her cape close and headed for the doctor's library. At breakfast Mrs. Braddock had called with a message from Doctor Carey: "Please see me in the library at 7:45." Why? Mrs. Braddock didn't know why. Life at Mercy was filled with the unexpected, but Julia was genuinely puzzled.

The book stacks reached from floor to ceiling, volumes on every area of medicine, the usual, the very rare. Julia felt as if she trod on hallowed ground.

Dr. Carey waited by the narrow nave window at the far end of the room. He turned, looked at her intently and said good morning. "Sit down, Miss Rogers, you look tired."

"I am, Dr. Carey, but it's a good tiredness. I'm on Obstetrics now and we had two deliveries—one was a friend from my high school days. Working to overcome her fear, I discovered how important a nurse's help can be."

"The nurse, the doctor, and the patient," Dr. Carey smiled, "to practice medicine successfully it takes all three." He settled back in a big leather chair.

Julia looked at the old doctor's spruce intense figure. He

79

was old, as his snow-white hair, bent fingers, and weary slump attested. But she recalled the first day she'd seen him operate. In the long gown he moved swiftly, with the energy and ease of a man whose body is the servant of his nimble mind. His bent fingers grew agile, sure, as they moved to accomplish. Skilled hands stay young.

"What do you hear from your family?"

"Oh, Mom writes every week. John's a sophomore now, and having trouble with Latin. Mike is impatient for Christmas, of course. Everyone's fine."

"I'm glad your mother writes regularly. How often do you write?"

Julia hesitated, tugged at her cape, avoided the doctor's eyes. "I write when I can. Of course I'm busy with classes, and. . . ."

"When did you write last?"

"This is December 10th, let's see. . . ." She tried to sound off-hand, casual. She meant to write often. "November? No, it must have been October, some time in October. But my mother understands, Dr. Carey."

"Perhaps so, but your brothers don't." He took a folded paper from his pocket, and read:

Dear Dr. Carey,
If our sister Julia Rogers is diseased please send her body to us at this address.
Michael and John Rogers

With just a hint of amusement Dr. Carey added, "I'm sure they mean 'deceased.' Someone should tell them you're quite alive. Shall I write or will you?"

"Oh, I'll write this very morning, Dr. Carey. I'm so sorry to have you involved."

80

Dr. Carey laughed, "Don't be, Julia. All the Mercy girls are sort of daughters to me."

Julia's fingers caressed the embroidered MH design on her cape, a replica of the school pin. "Sometimes I doubt that I'll ever know enough to wear a graduate's pin."

"Of course you will. But I can't say much for the pin itself. M.H. What does that say? Nothing. It could stand for Mata Hari or Minnehaha. I'd like to see the Mercy girls have a pin that symbolizes the real meaning of nursing." A clock at the far end of the room chimed the hour, and Dr. Carey stood. "Well, I didn't mean to keep you so long. You need your rest. Straight to bed, young lady."

Julia grinned. "Yes sir, but do you mind if I write a letter first? I do like to keep in touch with my family."

Dr. Carey chuckled. "Aren't you ashamed, Julia? Tricking a tired old man with his own words. Go along now."

Was it wrong to forget the yesterdays and give her attention and affection to this moment's need? Julia found the answer the following night. The night before she had given strength to Betsy, but that need was ended. It wasn't a matter of forgetting, but rather a moving forward. Every patient, every step of her nursing made her more able to cope with the new demand. Julia needed all her yesterdays for the night that she would always remember as very, very special.

It began at 11:20. Report was barely ended when the telephone rang. Head nurse, Mrs. Watts, answered, listened for a long moment, and said, "Yes, I can arrange it. We're not busy and I have two students. All right, Doctor." She pulled a new chart from the rack. "Miss Rogers, Dr. Johnson is bringing up a patient. You will stay with her as long as you're needed. Miss Thomas and I will take care of the rest of the patients."

Before Julia could do more than wonder, the flipflop of the doors called her to the far end of the corridor. At first glance Joe and Jane Murray seemed quite ordinary, both in their early thirties although they clung together just like the teen-age couples. Julia sensed something unusual.

Dr. Johnson took one hand of the small, pale woman, looked directly at her and said very slowly, "Jane, this is Miss Rogers, one of our finest nurses. She will be with you tonight."

Doctors seldom said such things and Julia's puzzlement grew. Jane made no answer but turned bewildered, beseeching eyes to her dark-haired husband.

Dr. Johnson said, "Explain to her, Joe, that Miss Rogers will take care of her now and that you'll see her again in a few minutes."

Joe raised his hands and in swift movements repeated the message in sign language. A deaf-mute—Jane's world was one of a cruel, lasting silence. As a child would, with confidence and trust, she put out her hand. Julia took it, gave it a warm little squeeze, and led Jane down the long corridor to Labor Room One.

As she prepared the patient, Julia worked slowly, pantomiming an explanation of each procedure and pausing often to smile or to pat the hand that lay clenched on the pillow. Then she raised her fingers in a gesture that said "I'll be right back," and went to call Joe Murray.

Joe went to his wife as though their separation had been intolerably long. He touched her fingers to his lips and caressed a stray strand of hair from her forehead.

Dr. Johnson waited for Julia in the hall. They looked at each other for a long moment without speaking. Then she said, "Jane will be all right, Doctor. Don't worry." A second-year student nurse reassuring a man who had completed his residency and opened his own office? Under most circumstances her words would be called impertinent but he took them as a bond of understanding.

"Thank God the supervisor could spare you, Miss Rogers. A constant flow of strange faces would upset Jane. I thought of ordering a private nurse but they can't afford it."

"If you'd like to lie down in the doctors' room, I'll call you in plenty of time, sir."

"No, I told Jane I'd stay with her and I shall."

Julia marveled at the man's infinite patience and at Jane's sustaining strength through the night's long hours. There wasn't much conversation. But the oneness of husband, wife, doctor, and nurse made words unnecessary.

Medically, the labor and delivery were uncomplicated. The baby girl's healthy cry proved that her care would be routine. But Jane and Joe and tiny Tressa were special to Julia because they were so special to each other. The unspoken intensity of feeling between Joe and Jane brought tears to Julia's eyes, and she felt privileged indeed to have shared this night with them.

No one voiced the question haunting them all: would Tressa share her mother's silent world or her father's noisy vocal one? It would be days before tests could prove her hearing or the lack of it.

As she went off duty Julia stopped by the tiny chapel. Twisting the prayer card in her pocket she implored the Creator of Life to allow this child the gift of hearing and the gift of speech. She realized now as never before that speech and hearing and sight were gifts. But the greatest gift was a love like Joe and Jane's. She sighed, wondering when her love and Paul's would grow to such height, such depth. It would have to, because now she couldn't settle for less.

12

Vigil

Christmas was divided for Julia. Since the twenty-fifth was midweek, she went home the weekend before for an early holiday celebration with the family. For the day itself she was invited to Phil and Betsy's apartment (where she went daily to bathe the baby and help with his formula). Shopping was done by dibs and dabs—the pigskin wallet for Paul had to be mailed in early December to ensure arrival, Rosemary's came next so she could mail it to the state hospital where one group of juniors was having psychiatric training. The family shopping was done in a dozen trips to Market Street, each one an exhausting delightful excursion into the wonderworld of a tinseled, bauble-bedecked San Francisco. Gifts for Phil, Betsy, and baby Paul were last-minute rush. It was nearly seven P.M. on the twenty-fourth when Julia reached the nurses' home, parcels stacked to her freckled nose, face aglow from the fresh cold wind off the Pacific. Her mail slot bulged with cards, two packages, and a folded note from Ma Marsh with a telephone call to be returned. While she waited for the telephone Julia opened the small flat package and found two exquisite handkerchiefs edged with handmade spidery lace and a card signed: Jane, Joe, and Tressa. For a moment Julia was back in one of the maternity rooms on that cold gray morning ten days before. If the sun forgot to shine outside that day it shone inside when Tressa's hearing ability was proved. Jane and Julia laughed and cried together, and Dr. Johnson beamed like a high-powered surgical lamp.

The other package was from Paul and contained a gold ring set with a shimmering pearl. For a moment Julia was tempted to put the ring on her left third finger but the card said simply: "Merry Christmas, darling." She slipped it on her right hand. Then the telephone was free.

The number was a Yukon exchange and totally unfamiliar, but the answering voice was not.

"Troy! What a nice surprise."

"Hi, Julie. Merry Christmas Eve! I called to ask if we could have dinner together tomorrow."

She explained about Betsy and Phil and offered her thanks for the Archers' invitation.

"Archer, singular," he corrected. "Lou Ellen's at the state hospital and the folks are in Palm Springs so Mom can sunbake a cold she's been fighting for weeks. I invented some elaborate plans for a week of skiing at Dodge Ridge so Mom would agree to their trip. I would have called you days earlier but I thought you were with Lou Ellen's group."

"Troy . . . Troy, may I call you back in a few minutes?" When he agreed Julia called Betsy, then called Troy again. "Betsy says to warn you this is her first turkey, but you're cordially invited."

"Oh, I couldn't, Julie."

"Well, you'd better, sir, because I volunteered us as the dishwashers."

Christmas morning at ten o'clock Troy called for Julia

at the nurses' home. He was still as tan as after his summer in Mexico, his smile wide and appreciative at the sight of her in her holly green suit dress. His obvious pleasure evoked a haunting phrase in Julia's mind. Wish I may, wish I might. She twisted the pearl ring in nervous circles.

He took her hand, noted the ring. "From Santa?"

Julia blushed, and nodded.

Troy reached for her coat. "Shall we go, princess? The coach and four await at the curb."

As they were leaving Ma Marsh called to Julia. "The telephone operator checked that number and it's not out of order. I guess your folks just aren't home this morning."

"Thanks, Ma." Julia let Troy help carry the stack of gifts and explained, "I've been calling every half hour but no one's home. I don't understand why." She tried to push worry away. "I'll try again at Betsy's."

Julia had to manage her gifts on the stairs to the apartment because Troy had a stack of his own, a bow-topped football for the baby, red carnations and candy for the Smiths, and a small star-crusted package marked "Julie." As she reached the landing Julia wondered what Phil and Betsy would think of her dating Troy when they knew she and Paul had a sort of understanding. They might not approve but they'd like Troy. Troy was so . . . so likable.

Julia needn't have been concerned because the next few minutes were a tumble of confusion, without time for appraisal, approval, or introductions. Betsy met them at the door with a frantic, "Hurry, Julia. The phone. Your mother. Something's happened!"

Julia jumped to the conclusion that the "something" had happened to her mother. She raced to the phone, slid on a small throw rug, spilled the gifts, bruised her knee on the table, bumped the phone to the floor, and nearly fainted with relief when her mother's voice came through the ear-piece, asking, "Julia, you all right?"

"Yes, Mom. What's wrong? Is it Dad? Mike? John? I've been trying to call you. What's wrong?"

In her calm, deliberate way Mary Rogers explained that Paul's father had had a serious heart attack about six A.M. and his condition was critical. "The Red Cross is arranging emergency leave for Paul and I think you should come home. I hate to spoil Betsy's dinner but—"

"Oh, poor Mr. Hammond. And poor Paul. Of course I'll come, Mom. Are you at home now?"

"No, Daddy and I are still at the hospital. Mr. Hammond doesn't have anyone until Paul gets here so I thought we'd better stay. The boys are with the Wilmingtons across the street, you know, Joe Wilmington is Mike's age. Daddy will drive up for you if you like, but the bus would be quicker."

"The bus will be fine. I'll meet you at the hospital. Bye, Mom."

Troy would not hear of her going home by bus. After a brief conversation with Betsy and Phil, he took her to pick up an overnight bag and a couple of uniforms. With Mrs. Braddock's permission, Julia was excused from duty for a few days and they were off on the hundred-mile drive to San Dorcas.

Along the humming freeway, over golden, gently rolling hills, through the green Santa Cruz mountains, Troy was his charming best, silent when Julia needed silence and cheerful without the false don't-worry undertone. Each time her tension showed in a tight little smile he came up with a remark so nonsensical that she had to smile a genuine smile. Shortly after one o'clock Julia was in uniform, a welcome supplement to the short-handed hospital staff. Much later she learned that Troy's afternoon was spent hosting John and Mike at a turkey dinner at the San Dorcas Inn. For the next critical, crucial thirty hours Julia's one concern was Arthur Hammond. For ten years he had been father and mother to Paul. He must live.

The next afternoon, Julia showered and put on a fresh uniform. Fresh makeup could not hide the dark circles from an almost sleepless night. But what matter? Mr. Hammond's tortured heart had settled to a quiet rhythm and, having survived the first, worst day and night, he had a chance. "Paul's coming," she had told him a hundred times over. And for a little while his confusion and panic would ease, only to begin again. "Paul's coming," she told him at four o'clock and again at five.

And then Paul was there. Weary and rumpled, white-faced with worry, Paul was there. After a long reassuring embrace with his father, Paul turned to her, held her at arm's length, then hugging her close, buried his face in her hair. "Oh, Julia, thank God you're here. We need you so much and you're here. Aren't we lucky you're a nurse!"

13

Comfort Me With Apples

Only once in her training did reassignment take Julia away from her own hospital. Change from one floor to another was abrupt, often unwelcome, but always a necessary step in her growing scope of skills. No change loomed larger than this one.

There was a certain excitement in packing and preparing for the trip. It was not a long one, just two hours, but the bus went north, though not as far north as the redwood country and east, but not as far east as the Sierra. Her destination lay in a summer hot, winter cold valley where wine grapes grew and "the hospital" was not where you went with a fracture or pneumonia. The hospital was called "State" by student nurses though it had a longer official name. To some patients it was a refuge, to others it was a jail, the bars of which were mental, not iron. To some it was a place to regain balance and reason. To others it was nothing, for they had lost contact with the real, and the road back was not a clear marked highway but a tricky maze.

Woven into Julia's excitement at her assignment to "State" were many threads of emotion. One was fear, fear of a new place, a type of nursing quite unlike anything she had done before and that other fear that is the shame of civilization, the fear that once caused the mentally ill to be burned as witches or brutally beaten to rid them of their "devils."

Another thread was weariness of routine—the routine of classes and floor time, of tests and hospital food, of baths and backrubs, of admissions and discharges, of doctor's orders and charts, of television in the recreation room and coffee in the kitchen. Each day, each patient different but somehow much alike.

The last thread was hope—hope that a change of scene would, by some magic, resolve her confusion of feelings. The confusion did not begin with Paul's return, but she pinpointed it there. Paul's love had poured forth first in words of gratitude, gratitude that she could and did give his father such capable loving care. He had at last understood the meaning of that undefinable word "nurse." His eyes mirroring his pride in her, he moved the pearl ring to her left hand.

What he could not understand was her willingness to leave his father later that week when the crisis was passed. "Mercy doesn't need you but Dad does," he argued. She failed to convince him that general duty care was sufficient for Mr. Hammond and that she needed Mercy and the remaining nineteen months of Mercy's training. Paul was hurt, and his hurt made the ring on her finger only what it had been in a shopkeeper's window, a lovely ornament. She went home every weekend in January, uniforms and duty shoes in her overnight case. Paul appreciated this but at each late Sunday leavetaking his eyes asked *"Why?"* When his emergency leave ended and he was assigned to San Diego he flew home each week. Through February Julia spent her days off at Mercy studying for exams and writing her case studies. Paul's letters came regularly, but they were more

90

like clinical reports than letters to be tied in love's pink ribbon. The pearl, which she could not move to her right hand but did not belong on her left, became as irritating to Julia as it had once been to the oyster.

Troy, too, contributed to her confusion. Early in January, Julia stopped by to see Betsy and found, forgotten in the excitement of that Christmas morning, the star-crusted package marked "Julie." Opening it she discovered a small flacon of perfume, a very proper sort of gift, but the label read *True Love*. Betsy giggled and said, "You've got a problem, girl. The way he looked at you and now this!"

Julia answered, "Don't be silly, Betsy. True love doesn't come in a bottle." She had tried to laugh, but tears crowded her throat. "Anyway Troy's no problem because I'm engaged to Paul." She lifted her left hand to prove it.

Betsy's reply was motherly and gentle. "Julia, engagement doesn't happen to your finger. It happens to your heart."

"State" was almost that—a self-sufficient place sprawled over forty acres, with its own power plant, fire department, churches, library, shops, theater, laundry, wide tree-lined avenues and buses with scheduled stops at each of the forty ward buildings. The administrative building was adobe with foot-thick walls and hand-hewn shake shingles. The other buildings, sand-colored stucco with red tiled roofs and stone walkways, showed the Spanish influence of early California. Julia came and saw and was conquered—by eucalyptus that reached high in the clear blue sky, by ancient gray-green oaks, by an atmosphere so calm and quiet that one could almost hear the opening of the spring-awakened iris buds.

Here the students from Mercy met affiliates from a dozen other hospitals and shared with them the nurses' residence where the rooms were singles, comfortable but as impersonal as a hotel. Julia longed for the homeliness of the bile-green room at Mercy, Rosemary's bubbly chatter, and the heavy thump of Ma's feet on the stairs.

The days were filled with patients and classes. Psychiatry's language must be learned: dementia, melancholia, repression, megalomania, paranoid, id, ego, compensation, euphoria—strange words that became keys to understanding these people in crisis, some of whom Julia would never forget.

Homely, pixie-like Ethel whose contentment depended on a one-eared rabbit, a rag doll, and a pair of high-topped tennis shoes, had a name for each of the nurses. Because of her freckles, Julia was dubbed "Spatterface." Lois Evans she called "Waddlefoot," for no known reason. She called the supervisor "Eyeballs."

Mr. Sam, on Male Admitting, confided his problem to Julia. One night while he was sleeping, the FBI wired his brain so they could tune in on all his thoughts and steal his inventions. He promised Julia half the worth of his electrical diasmoscoptic coordinator if she would get an electrician to unwire him.

Not once did Julia meet a patient who thought himself Napoleon, but she met many who considered themselves God. The faces of some seemed a diary of all the slain hopes and hurts of their past. Other faces were empty, as unlifelike as mannequins, from some came an endless flow of words, others did not speak.

One morning gray-haired, grandmotherly Mrs. Webb said hello to Julia, the first word she had uttered in five years. That one word repaid the hours Julia had spent talking to her while they played cards, worked at the rug loom, or fitted a jigsaw puzzle. "Hello." Only two syllables. Said in two seconds. To most people, a word spoken automatically.

But for Mrs. Webb it was a giant step, a conscious effort toward a world she had rejected. Julia hoped this signaled a quick, easy cure, but in psychiatry nothing is quick and nothing is easy. Another nurse, weeks later, would bring forth her first full sentence. Only then could a doctor begin the slow unraveling of her tangled mind. Cure depended upon insight, insight required communication, communication began with one word. Hello.

Julia found the senile ward less hopeful. Here minds were at the mercy of merciless time. Gentle old ladies wandered in a yesterday world recalling to each other happenings of forty, fifty, sixty years ago but they could not remember what month this was or what they ate for breakfast. They could not live in the outside world because they wandered physically as well as mentally. State could not offer them cure but it gave shelter, care and protection.

Group therapy sessions were a time of learning. The circle of chairs held six patients, one psychiatrist, and one nurse. At first Julia thought the conversations among the group were like conversations in any group of people. She soon learned that the talk was not allowed to meander aimlessly this way and that, but was skillfully directed into useful channels, occasionally by the nurse, most often by the doctor. In each case the object was the same: help the patient recognize and face his problem. The tea-party pleasant beginning lasted only until a blunt word bruised someone's feelings, setting off an hour-long explosion of words.

Julia picked for her case study brusque, poetry-quoting thirty-five-year-old Mattie Hamilton. At first glance, one might think Mattie belonged in a meeting of executive directors instead of a group therapy session. Indeed, her name had once been lettered in gold on her office in a large company, but that was when her decisions affected the lives of others, not her own. In the sessions Mattie showed a

remarkable ability to hit at the heart of the problem, anyone's problem including her own. *Stay me with flagons, comfort me with apples, for I am sick of love*—she quoted from
Solomon because she could not resolve the conflict of loves:
the demands of her invalid mother and her fiance's insistence
on setting a wedding date. Tranquilizers controlled her
tears and tremors, but that was only a beginning. She would
not be well until she could make a choice and live with it.

Julia's case study concluded with a hopeful prediction
for Mattie Hamilton: her intelligence and self-understand-
ing promise a rapid recovery.

But Mattie was still there when Julia's time at State
ended in late May. As she took one last look from the bus
window Julia thought of Mattie and wondered when, if
ever, she could leave. Why couldn't she decide what to do
and then do it? As the bus rolled west toward the opal-
streaked sunset, Julia twisted Paul's ring around and around.
One thing she had learned at State: ignoring the problem
didn't make it go away. With a painful tug at her heart
as well as her finger, she removed the pearl ring and put
it in her handbag. It would have to go back to Paul. It
would, by tomorrow's mail.

See, Mattie? You just decide what has to be done and do
it.

Lois Evans, sitting next to Julia, said, "I'm starved.
Good thing I stopped at the canteen before we left. How
about you, Rogers? Want an apple?"

Julia thanked her and bit hard into the crisp cold fruit.
Her taste buds pronounced it delicious, her diet classes
assured her it was nutritious, but Oh Mattie you were
wrong: for the pain of love there is no comfort in apples.

14

Special Delivery

"Waffles again?" Mike complained. "How come Julia always wants waffles, Mama?"

"Because hospitals don't serve waffles and since this is Julia's vacation we cook what she likes." Mary Rogers poured batter on the griddle and closed the lid.

"It's my vacation, too," he replied, as forlorn as a nine-year-old could manage on a bright and beautiful June morning.

"So it is," Mrs. Rogers said. "What would you like for breakfast, sir?"

Mike rubbed his freckled nose, ran his hand over the stubble of his crewcut, and considered. Timing his answer to Julia's appearance at the kitchen door, he solemnly announced, "Waffles."

Even after a full week of vacation, Julia felt like a guest in the house. At Mercy when her reactions puzzled her she could talk them out in a seminar session and come to understand not only her emotions but the patient's reactions, too. Employing the same technique she blamed her "guest feeling" on the fact that the family had moved to a rambling old house on the outskirts of San Dorcas and she had had no part in the decision or the selection. Here there was room for Mike's new collie pup, for John to raise rabbits, for rows of corn and beans, a rose garden, a hammock between two pines. But nowhere was there a space or a spot that said "Julia lives here, too." Even the toothbrush holder had only four resident spaces so hers stood in a tumbler, a visitor.

"Julia!"

"Yes, Mom."

"Mike is talking to you."

"I'm sorry, Mike. I guess I was day-dreaming. What did you want?"

"I forget now. Boy, Julia, I thought you were different, but you're not. You're just as dopey as ever, standing around staring at nothing." He reached for the syrup, and bumped his juice over. "Now I remember. I mixed the orange juice this morning."

Julia felt suddenly and completely at home. As she sponged the puddle on the table, she laughed and said, "Great job, funnyface."

"Same to you, dopey sister."

"No, I mean the mixing, not the spilling."

"Oh, thanks. You want to go swimming today, Julia?"

"I'd like to, Mike, but I promised Paul I'd—"

"Boy, I wish he'd stayed in the Marines. We were having fun until he came home."

"Michael," Mrs. Rogers said, "that will be enough. If you're finished with your waffle, suppose you get your room straightened up and make your bed." When he made a reluctant exit, she turned to Julia. "How is Paul?"

Julia laughed. "When we were at State we did IPR's—Interpersonal Relations, which means we recorded and interpreted patient-nurse conversations. The finished IPR reads: "He said—he meant"; "I said—I meant"; and so forth. An IPR of this conversation would read: "She said, 'How's Paul' "—she meant, "Did you get the ring matter settled and what is Paul going to do now that he's discharged?"

Mrs. Rogers smiled. "There ought to be a law against children outsmarting their parents."

Julia refilled their coffee cups, stirred sugar into hers. "He gave me the pearl again, but not as an engagement ring. I don't know, Mom—for some reason Paul and I talk about everything but the things that matter. And we talk words, not feelings."

"Maybe you ought to do one of those IPRs of your conversations. Anyway, he's been home only a few hours. It takes time to build rapport." Mrs. Rogers stacked the breakfast dishes and sat down. Before she had more than one swallow of coffee, Mike bounced in, his transistor radio in one hand, the mail in the other. At his heels, the collie pup waggled for attention.

Julia shuffled through the envelopes, handed all but one to her mother. Out of habit she reached for her bandage scissors, then fingered open the flap and scanned the single page. "Letter from Troy—oh, Mom, he says he's driving to Los Angeles on business and plans to stop by to say hello to the family. Did I tell you he graduated from law school and he's now a junior associate in a San Francisco firm?"

"How very nice. Troy's one young man who knows where he's going."

Julia stiffened. "That's not fair, Mom. Paul hasn't really had time to decide what he's going to do."

"Don't be so defensive, Julia. We were discussing Troy, weren't we? Anyway, Paul's a fine boy and no one expects him to be as mature at twenty as Troy is at twenty-four."

"Well, it just isn't fair to compare them."

97

"Mama," Mike said, looking at his sister intently, "is Julia going to cry?"

"Of course not, Mike." Mrs. Rogers finished her coffee. "When is Troy coming?"

"Wednesday or Thursday, he says. Gosh—that's today or tomorrow. Guess it will be tomorrow, Mom. He'd have been here by now. Oh, look at the time. Paul will be here about eleven. I'll do up the dishes and get dressed."

"Maybe I should buy a couple of chickens in case Troy does get here today. If I'm nominated to entertain him, I'll do it with food. Or should I get a roast?"

The back-door screen banged, and John rushed in. "I'll bet today's the day, Mom."

"But his letter said today *or* tomorrow. John, would you check to see if we have enough charcoal for the barbecue?" Mrs. Rogers stopped suddenly. "Mike, put the pup outside and turn off that radio. Julia, hold the dish-rattling for a minute. Now, John, what are you talking about?"

"I think my rabbit will have her litter today. Gretchen's acting mighty funny, and Dad and I figured it would be one day this week."

"Good. I'm going shopping and Mike can help me. Julia, I guess you'll be with Paul by the time I get back. John, you'll want to stay with Gretchen, I imagine." She smiled at each of them. "Now, at the count of three, pandemonium may resume."

As the clatter and rattle of family activity began again, Julia hummed to herself. It was good to be home.

She was buttoning her blue denim wrap-around skirt below a red bandana blouse when the doorbell rang. With a quick line of lipstick she was ready. Picking up blue denim sneakers she padded barefoot down the steps and to the door. "Paul, come in. I'll be ready in a jiffy."

"Fine, darling. I have a big day planned for us." He

held her close as he kissed her. "Whom do you love?" he whispered.

"Paul Andrew Hammond," she answered in a chanted rhythm.

"Who loves you?"

"Paul Andrew Hammond."

"Whom will you marry?"

"Paul Andrew Hammond."

He lifted her, whirled her in dizzying circles, his hug growing tighter and tighter. "Oh, Julia, I'm bursting with news. Dad and I talked for hours last night and wait till you hear our plans." He let her feet touch the floor, scooped up her dropped shoes and followed her, laughing and breathless, to the living room. While she slid into her sneakers his news bubbled out. "We checked with the doctor, and he said Dad's well enough to make a trip and what a trip we have planned—Dad's going to sell his business, and we'll buy a pickup with a camper and a vacation trailer. We'll go everywhere—a tour of all the states and Canada— maybe Mexico too. Oh, Julia, we'll have a honeymoon to end all honeymoons—we'll take a whole year and go everywhere. The most leisurely trip you can imagine. And Dad even let me have my mother's diamond for your engagement ring—I think he loves you as much as I do, Julia. And we won't have to worry about his diet or medicine or anything because you can take care of all that."

Julia, fidgeting with a stubborn shoelace, could hardly believe her ears. She looked up at him, her throat as knotted as the shoe tie. "Paul, you don't mean—"

"Yes, Julia, I mean every word. Isn't it fabulous! If you'll get those shoes on, we'll go pick up the ring. The jeweler will have it ready at noon."

"Paul, I can't."

He stood, drew her to her feet, tilted her chin up until

their eyes met. He smiled the sweet disarming smile she could never resist and began the old familiar patter. "Whom do you love?"

Julia could not answer. A honeymoon with Paul and his father? Plans all made.

"Say yes, Julia. Just say yes."

She buried her face in the soft green of his sport shirt. I'm drowning, she thought. Drowning in a sea of words and plans. The hospital, a nursing career seemed a million miles away and Paul was here, holding her close, waiting for her "yes." But a "yes" to him was a "no" to everything else. "Paul, I think we should talk this over."

"What's to say, Julia? Everything is set. All you have to do is say 'yes.' "

Anger, hot and furious, swelled within her. "Didn't it even occur to you that I would like to be in on the planning? You don't know what you're asking." She pulled away, gripping her hands behind her to keep from slapping his confident smile, his neat little package of plans, his honeymoon for three.

"What's the problem, Julia?"

"If you have to ask, I couldn't explain to you in a million years."

"Julia, will you talk sense?"

The chime of the doorbell spared her the necessity of an answer. Her blue eyes still flashing, her breath crowding past the tears of anger balled in her throat, she flung open the door. On the porch stood Troy Archer.

"Hi, Julie. I'd have been here earlier but I didn't know you'd moved."

"Sis! Sis!" John's screams came from the back of the house. "Julia! Where *are* you?"

"Here, John, in the front hall," she called. As she invited Troy inside, Paul came from the living room. There was

100

no time for introductions because John, face white with panic, rushed in and pulled at Julia. "She's dying, Sis! I think Gretchen's dying. She's just lying there, all funny looking."

"Who's Gretchen?" Troy asked.

"The kid's fool rabbit," Paul said.

John shot a look of sheer loathing at Paul. He gulped to control his anger. "Please, Sis, come see."

Julia put one hand on his shoulder. "Calm down, John. First of all, have any of the babies arrived yet?"

"No."

Troy asked, "Is this her first litter?" At John's nod, he went on, "And this is your first experience?" Again John nodded. "Let's go take a look. Maybe it's not all that bad."

With a grateful smile John led the way. Julia turned to follow, but Paul's arm detained her.

"The boy vet is going to the rescue, Julia. I told the jeweler we'd be there at noon."

Julia, chin high, said, "I'm going to see about Gretchen."

Paul shrugged and followed.

They found Troy with his arm across John's shoulder, watching the rabbit's labored breathing and looking helpless.

"Something *is* wrong, Julie," Troy said. "John says the veterinarian is out of town. I don't know what to do."

Julia reached inside the wire hutch, stroked the gray fur tenderly and laid her hand on the bulging side of the doe. She considered a moment, then hesitantly offered, "I could perform a Cesarean. The babies are alive. I can feel them move."

John hesitated. "I don't know, Sis. Gretchen's so weak."

Paul said, "You do fine as a nurse, Julia, but you're not a vet."

She turned to her brother. "I'm not a veterinarian, John,

but you're going to lose Gretchen either way. I may be able to save the babies. What do you think?"

John, taller than Julia, measured her, his eyes coming to rest on her slim fingers. "Operate, Sis. We've got to do something. Just do your best."

"Tell me what I can do to help, Julie," Troy said.

She looked around the sunny backyard. "We'll use the patio table and I'll need some newspapers to cover it. In the garage, Troy—you'll see the stack. John, you get Mom's sharp-pointed sewing scissors and a towel." John raced toward the house.

Troy came back with the newspapers. "What else will you need?"

"A box, I guess. A shoe box. John will know where to find one. And some cotton—in the medicine chest of the upstairs bathroom."

"Will do!" Troy sprinted off across the lawn.

"May I ask who Helpful Henry is?" Paul folded his arms, waiting for her answer.

"Troy Archer, a friend of the family. Didn't I introduce you?"

"No, you didn't. Julia, let's go before you start this girl-surgeon bit. You'll get all involved and John will blame you."

"Oh, but I am involved, Paul—I'm part of a family. I'm a nurse. I'm a woman, and right now John needs a woman's help. You want me to marry you, but you don't even know me. Now if you'll move aside, I have work to do."

"Julia, you've changed. I don't know why, but you've changed."

"Yes, Paul, I have, and you haven't. That's the problem. I hope you and your father enjoy the trip."

"Now why do you say a dumb thing like that? We're

all going. Unless you mean you're not—not going to marry me? You'd better be sure, Julia Rogers, because if I leave I won't be back. There are lots of other fish in the sea, you know."

A light bubble of laughter escaped her lips. "So go fishing, Paul."

She watched him stride across the grass to the side gate and disappear around the corner of the house. She had watched him leave before with tears in her eyes, but this time she felt only a small regret because, in spite of fifteen years as neighbors and five years of going together, they were parting as strangers.

Julia spread the papers on the tables, weighted the corners with garden rocks. John and Troy brought the necessary equipment.

"Now bring Gretchen," she directed John. Her calm assurance steadied him and he tenderly lifted the sleek rabbit from her pen and laid her on the table in front of his sister.

Julia looked at Troy, consternation clouding her eyes.

He glanced from her to Gretchen to John. "Julie," he said. "We have everything but the hot water."

"Let me get it, Sis. How much?"

"A teakettle full, John, and be sure it's boiling."

"I'll bring it as soon as it starts to steam." John streaked to the house.

Troy whispered, "You'd better hurry, Julie. Gretchen has stopped breathing."

She nodded and picked up the sharp pointed scissors.

Five minutes later she carried the shoe box to the back door. "John."

"The water isn't boiling yet. I'm trying to hurry it, Sis."

"Never mind, John. I guess we won't need it." She

103

handed him the box, watched his face reflect worry, disbelief, relief, and total happiness. Four tiny hairless bunnies curled together in their cotton nest.

"Sis, you did it, you really did it. Boy, how many guys have a sister who could do this!"

Julia glowed with pleasure. "They'll have to be kept warm and out of drafts. When Mom comes we'll ask her if we can use the heating pad."

"How'll we feed them, Sis?" he asked, sure now that Julia had all the answers.

"I wish I had a Breck feeder from the hospital but an eyedropper will do. I'll ask Troy to drive down to the drugstore so we can buy a couple."

"Do you know what, Julia? I like that Troy. He's a great guy."

As she turned to leave she said, "For once, John, I agree with you."

The patio table was bare. Smoke curled from the incinerator. Troy was nowhere in sight.

"Troy, where are you?"

"Here in the garage, Julie. I'm putting away your dad's shovel."

"The shovel. Did you . . ."

"Yes, under the lilac bush. You can tell John later, if he asks."

She watched as he hung the shovel among the tools on the garage wall. He wiped his forehead, shoved the handkerchief in his back pocket.

"Is anything wrong, Julie? You keep staring at me. Is my face dirty?"

"No," she said. "I was thinking how very nice you are."

Grinning, he opened his arms to her. She went to him, raised her face for his kiss. A long minute later, he touched her cheek, her hair with caressing fingers. "Something tells

104

me I've won this case by default, but a lawyer never argues a ruling in his favor." His arms closed around her.

"I'm not here by court order, sir. If you're looking for a reason, you might say it's de fault of de rabbit." Troy groaned and kissed her freckled nose. In one voice they said, "I love you."

At that moment John dashed into the garage. "Mom's home and she's got an eyedropper. Holy Cow! You two playing Post Office?"

Troy grinned. "Sure, John. Special Delivery."

John's ears flamed. "I kinda feel like kissing her myself, but it's kinda goofy to kiss your own sister."

"Never mind, John," Troy said in his best legal voice. "I'll do it for you."

15

New Directions

"Here we are, Miss," the driver announced as the taxi ground to an abrupt stop before the nurses' home. Julia gave the brick and ivy-covered dormitory a look of warm welcome. Third floor, second floor, and in another month she'd move to a first-floor senior room. A senior. Imagine. The driver cleared his throat politely and Julia looked up. He'd been standing by the open door, waiting while she daydreamed. With an embarrassed laugh, she gathered her makeup case, the package of homemade cookies, and a last-minute gift from John, a framed picture of the four bunnies. She fumbled for her wallet.

"Never mind the money, Miss, I've been wantin' to do you a good turn. You took care of me when I had my hernia operation last year. You did a good job, too. I haven't had a bit of trouble since. I told the wife if I ever got the chance, I'd give you a free lift."

Julia looked into the broad, weathered face, hoping for some clue of identity.

"Didn't think you recognized me, Miss, you not speakin' when you got into the cab. I guess we don't look the same, in clothes." Now it was his turn for embarrassment and they laughed together. "My wife's comin' here in November for our second baby. Hope you'll be on the Maternity Floor then."

"I'm afraid I won't Mister . . . Mister . . . I'm sorry. I just can't think of your name."

"Gruzaninski, John Gruzaninski. You'll be watchin' for my missus in November. Okay?"

She grinned agreement, aware that an attempt to explain the assignment system would prove futile. "I can handle my suitcase, Mr. Gruzaninski. Thank you for the ride and say hello to your wife for me."

The cab rolled away and Julia stood looking for a moment at the pale circle of the late June moon. The months of treading Mercy's corridors had accounted for many patients and she wondered how many she'd passed unknowing, how many had waited for her to say hello. Each had been entered on her nursing record, but only as a diagnosis. That wasn't the kind of nurse she wanted to be. Diagnosis and room number were important, but first of all came the patient, the human individuality.

She picked up the suitcase and ambled slowly up the walk. Lois opened the door and Julia stepped into the foyer. She glanced at a group of students gathered in the living room and sang out, "What's this, a reception committee for lil' old me? I didn't know you missed me, gals. I didn't know you cared."

The quiet of the room held unbroken. Only faint smiles of greeting met hers and she blurted, "What is this? A convention of depressives? Or is this official frown week at Mercy?"

A voice behind her answered, "You must not have heard the news, Rogers."

Julia whirled around and faced a senior's sober expression. Her face felt stiff, the funny smile still in place. She turned again to the girls who sat in rigid solemn silence.

"Dr. Carey died today," said someone on the far side of the room.

Julia gasped in disbelief. Her suitcase dropped with a muffled thud. Tears welled inside her and made the rose figured draperies blur together like a child's finger painting.

Dr. Carey is dead!

The words hammered in her mind, as if repetition would bring realization. Dr. Carey, as much a part of Mercy as the mortar between the bricks, as old as winter and as young as spring, just couldn't be dead.

"What happened?" The words squeezed past the ache in her throat.

Everyone talked at once, then no one talked. Finally Lois told the few details. He'd been doing a bone graft, long and tedious, and when he finished, he'd walked from the operating room, sat down at the desk in the hallway and died.

Conversation came from all sides now.

"You know Dr. Carey, he never would leave a thing half done."

"Coronary occlusion, that's what Dr. Johnson diagnosed. He was assisting and didn't realize anything was wrong until Dr. Carey walked out."

"If ever a man died with his boots on!"

"I sure wouldn't want to be the one to tell those kids at San Estaban."

"Do you remember the time. . . . ?"

The room hummed with murmured memories as the sad-hearted girls spoke an eloquent eulogy of this man who served his Maker and mankind with exquisite tenderness.

Julia's thoughts went back to the many times she had made rounds with him, cared for his patients, scrubbed for his surgery, dipped plaster rolls as he applied a cast.

When her throat felt too full to bear, she raced from the room, out into the blackness of the night. The path to the hospital, well known through sun and rain, through mist and blanking fog, lay beneath her feet and she let it lead her to the quiet coolness of the chapel. There, kneeling before the dimly lit crucifix, Julia gave way to her tears and her lips moved in prayer.

When she returned to her room, she found Rosemary still in uniform, though she had been off duty for hours.

"Hi, Julia. I guess you heard about Dr. Carey." Her eyes, usually a merry blue, were dark with tears. "I scrubbed for him today. I still can't believe he's . . . gone." She held back a sob. "He was telling us about the kids at San Estaban—you know the hospital for crippled children. And he said Mercy graduates could always count on a job there—he liked to see his Mercy girls taking care of his special kids. Then Dr. Johnson started talking about how the kids prize a Carey cast because he drew a cartoon face on each one and—oh, Julia. He had so much to give."

Julia nodded. "He was something different, something special to everyone who knew him."

Grief lingers, but the work of a hospital must never stop. Life at Mercy returned to its usual pace. Three days later, as twilight pushed away the last rays of the sun, Julia stood before the long mirror above the living room fireplace. She moved a step closer and turned her head just enough to see the reflection of the two narrow stripes, pressed in ebony precision on her cap. Satisfied that they were really there, really hers, she moved back to a clear space by the wall and watched in silence as Mrs. Braddock pinned in place the senior caps of her classmates. There was no speech, no ceremony. Those were saved for the real stars of to-

109

night's performance, the students who were now filing into the room, strangely quiet, awed by their custom-tailored white uniforms, hallmarks of their status as graduate nurses. Their heads were bare. The wide black stripes were not presented in the casual manner used for student stripes. Julia caught Sue Lambert's eye and smiled her congratulations.

Julia had never been to a school of nursing graduation, but she knew just how it would be. The large church dark save for the dramatic white tapers flanking the platform, the caps stacked neatly on a table to the right, the alabaster Nightingale lamps standing in a row to the left, the liquid beauty of the organ's voice filling the nave. Yes, she could close her eyes and see it all.

Rosemary, walking as though the new cap might fall and break, searched the crowded room and worked her way to Julia. "Hi, Senior! Ain't they purty?" She gave her cap a proud pat. "I pity the poor underclassmen, working three to eleven, so we can go to graduation."

"What's so bad about that, Rosie? We didn't mind last year when we worked so the upperclassmen could see their big sisters graduate. It doesn't seem possible that we're really seniors! It was yesterday that we started."

Rosemary wagged her head in disagreement. "Not for me. I feel I've been a nurse all my life. I guess I have been, all of my life that really matters. The years before were just there to get me old enough to be here."

"Oh, you don't mean that. You just feel that way because it's graduation night and all." Julia wondered at her roommate's bitter summation of past years.

"No, Julia, this is the first time I've accomplished anything worthwhile. I've never talked much about my mother. She's really a fine woman, but she still doesn't believe I'll finish. And what's worse she'd make all my excuses for me if I did quit. Don't tell me you didn't have an inkling of

110

this, Julia. Do you know anyone else who gets four letters a week from her mother? And two phone calls?"

Ma Marsh spoke over the buzz of conversation. "The buses are here, Mrs. Braddock."

Julia greeted the interruption with an audible sigh of relief. Her own happy family life made it difficult to understand a mother who expected, even encouraged, failure. Rosemary's I-can, I-will attitude saved her, but how many patients at State were there because they accepted a failure label? She felt a deep affection and admiration for Rosemary, but this was not the time to spell out her feelings.

The bus seats remained empty, the aisles crowded with standing nurses. There must be no seat-creases in uniforms worn to graduation. After a short ride along one edge of Golden Gate Park, a left turn and then a right, the buses swung into the church parking area.

As her class found its place near the front, Julia listened to the magnificent tone of the organ. She lacked the trained ear of a musician, but somehow the organ didn't sound quite as she imagined it would have under Dr. Carey's hands. The beginning of the ceremony cut short any melancholia.

The invocation by the white-haired clergyman, the bestowing of graduate caps and gold pins, the miniature candled lamps aglow as the young women repeated the Nightingale pledge . . . so went the ceremony, as old as the nursing profession, yet poignantly beautiful in its sameness.

Julia scarcely listened as the chairman of the Board of Directors of Mercy Hospital was introduced and began to speak. Her thoughts drifted back to her capping, scanned the years since, then hurried on to one year hence when she would graduate. Graduation was the end, and yet the beginning. The beginning of what, she wondered. Once she and Paul had planned each step of their future. Now her life

111

held only two certainties: she was beginning her third and best year at Mercy and her love for Troy was deep and sure.

"Dr. Carey!" The words cut through her reverie and caught her attention.

"I have long been aware of Dr. Carey's desire for a new pin for the graduates of Mercy Hospital, something that would be symbolic of the true meaning of nursing. In his will, Dr. Carey set aside a sum of money, underwriting the cost of changing the design. And who is more capable of planning this design than you nurses? You young women, students and graduates of Mercy, are the ones who know the meaning of nursing, for you live it every day. We ask that you submit your ideas and sketches to the Board. It is our hope that next graduation, in Dr. Carey's memory, a new symbol of Mercy will be a reality."

Julia remembered a chill winter morning and her conversation with the old doctor. She had almost forgotten his quick dismissal of the entwined MH emblem as meaningless. Now, as then, he sought a significant symbol, a pin with a meaning, for the school he loved.

The program of graduation, fast drawing to a close, was returned to Reverend Dunnigan. His voice filled the vast darkness although his words were addressed directly to the graduates.

"You have repeated your pledge of devoted care to the sick and suffering. I pray God's guidance for you in your chosen profession. And I ask that you remember that there is more to nursing than physical care. The spiritual side of man must not be forgotten. Reverence for life is the keystone of nursing. You who watch life aborning, you who close eyes in death, you who deal directly with human life, the most precious element on earth, must blend your skill and your knowledge with love, with compassion, with understanding. This is the spirit of nursing and in answer-

112

ing the call of the suffering, you are truly the handmaids of the Lord."

He spoke the benediction, but his words were lost to Julia. She was caught by the striking beauty of his hands, arresting, these hands of service. And somewhere in the back of her mind, the seed of an idea germinated.

16

Four Hands

"Mith Wo . . . gers!" The snub-nosed face pressed hard against the metal crib bars and frank blue eyes searched the glass windowed wards with veteran precision. "Mith Wogers!" The call grew louder, more insistent.

Julia poked her head in at the door of Ward B. "Be with you in a minute, Molly. Lie down now, little one." She returned to the routine of evening temperatures and the wards were quiet for a full five minutes before the lisping call began again. The last temperature noted, Julia urged tired feet to the crib where the appealing "Mith Wogers" originated.

"Now, little Miss Mischief, what can I do for you?"

The blue eyes stared accusingly. "I called you and called you. I wanted you now, Mith Wogers."

"You've got me now, Molly."

"No, I mean now before, not now in a minute."

"Molly Franklin, you're a rascal." Julia grinned at the serious air of this diminutive dictator.

"What's a wascal?"

"A rascal is a three-year-old-golly-gobble who thinks she's the only little girl in the whole ward."

"But I want you to hold me."

"Now, Molly we both know you're supposed to rest. How is your rheumatic fever going to get better if you're climbing out of bed all the time?"

"I could west weal well in your lap and we both know I'm sposed to west."

Julia conceded, reached for the battered rocker in the corner and carefully lifted the smiling youngster to her lap. The old chair creaked as the rockers began their lazy sway. Strong arms encircled the frail body as Molly snuggled close, her ear laid over Julia's heartbeat.

"You *are* my nurse, huh, Mith Wogers?"

"You've asked me that every day for three weeks, Molly. You're pretty hard to convince."

"But are you?"

Julia tucked the bare feet under the hem of the flannel gown and caressed wispy strands of caramel-colored hair in place. "Yes, little one. I'm *your* nurse."

"But sometimes you don't hold me when I ask you."

"Sometimes I just can't. Why, I'd need four hands to keep up with you and all the other children, too."

The snub nose wrinkled into a giggle. "You're funny, Mith Wogers. You'd be weally funny, if ya had four hands."

Julia lifted her young patient into bed and smoothed the covers with a tender motion. "Oh, I wouldn't show the extra hands to any one else. I'd keep them in my pockets until you called me."

"And you'd keep 'em just for me?"

Julia's answering nod brought a smile.

The shuffle of feet in the corridor signaled the beginning of visiting hours.

"Is your grandmother coming tonight?"

Molly's smile drained away. "Huh-uh! She called on the phone she's thick."

"Well, never mind, Molly. She'll be well soon, and she'll be so happy when she hears how well you're doing." She thumbed through a stack of worn books. "Here's your favorite kitty book."

Molly accepted the slim volume with a half-hearted smile. "Will you come back and hold me before sleepin' time?"

"I'll try, punkin, but I have a lot of medications to give. Now, let's see, where did I leave that extra pair of hands? Oh, here they are, right in my pockets."

A grin dimpled Molly's delicate cheeks and Julia walked from the ward.

At the nurse's station, a junior student sat before a desk piled high with charts. "Oh, there you are, Miss Rogers. The supervisor was just here with the new assignment sheet." Longing surged into her voice as she said, "You're assigned to Public Health and Visiting Nurse beginning Monday. Oh, Miss Rogers, aren't you thrilled!"

Julia's reaction was something less than enthusiastic. "I've been looking forward to it for ever so long, but. . . ." She regretted qualifying the statement. What could she say now but admit her more than professional devotion to the tiny Raggedy-Ann patient who constantly pressed the question, "Are you my nurse, Mith Wogers?" The convalescence of Molly Franklin had been uncomplicated and there was little damage to the heart. It wasn't her physical well-being that caused concern. It was the haunting need for reassurance, the too-old troubled sadness of the deep blue eyes.

"But what, Miss Rogers?"

"I was just thinking of Molly. She's so . . . well, so vulnerable. Her grandmother is sick. Her father is dead, and her mother skipped off to Los Angeles without even a good-bye. Hardly a situation to breed security for a three-year-old." Julia forced a little laugh, found it unconvincing. "I

116

guess I'm just the mother hen type. Being objective about the patients just isn't my forte."

Anxious to change the subject, Julia glanced at the heart-shaped doodlings on the telephone pad. "What's all this?"

The junior nurse ripped off the top page, crumpled it and tossed it in the wastebasket. "I was trying to come up with a pin design to submit before the December 1st deadline. The best I could do was a red heart with MH in gold. One of the freshmen submitted a sketch of block letters spelling out Mercy. I think that's a good idea."

"It is." Julia laughed. "My roommate suggested crossed thermometers behind a dull hypo. Anyway, you should turn in your idea. It's at least as good as the one I submitted."

"What was your suggestion?"

Before Julia could answer the plaintive "Mith Wogers" call began again.

At six-ten the following Monday morning, Julia stepped from the steamy fog of the shower and toweled off with a brisk see-saw of the husky linen. Thoughts of the coming day were crowded out by a review of yesterday's events. The leave-taking of young Molly had been almost too easy. She'd settled for a promise of regular visits, and seemed resigned to the here-to-day-and-gone-tomorrow adults who peopled her life.

Julia pulled on her corduroy robe, slid into fur-trimmed scuffs, and padded down the hall. The flip-flap of her slippers was lost in the corridor traffic.

Lou Ellen called, "You'd better wear your heavy raincoat, Julia. That November breeze sounds pretty sharp."

"Yes, Mother." Julia qualified her flippancy with a smile.

Their caps tucked safely into plastic bags, Julia and Lou Ellen found the outlying Public Health Clinic to which they were assigned. It was not nearly so impressive as the huge stone main Health Building in Civic Center but it

117

was neat, with fresh white paint and sparkling clean windows. Julia expected a noisy babbling crowd. The crowd was there but it was quiet, well ordered. A large stock of toys lay in scattered disarray on the shiny linoleum and a dozen children sprawled in concentrated enjoyment.

"Must be Well Baby Day," Lou Ellen observed dryly. "It's rather refreshing to see so many healthy specimens at once. After Pediatrics and Emergency, I thought children came in only two categories: hurt and hollering. Come on, let's see where we're supposed to go."

A smartly suited secretary appeared at the door near the reception desk. "Good morning, girls. Students from Mercy? I'll show you where to hang your coats and Miss Averill will take you from there."

Beyond the door lay six rooms, a doctor's office, two examining rooms, an X-ray room, a small lab, and a nurses' lounge, where a coffee pot was perking. Miss Averill, looking just-combed and neat in a navy blue cotton smock, welcomed the girls with a warm smile and hot coffee.

"This morning will be mostly routine," she began. "Vaccinations, immunizations, and counseling on Well Baby Care. We have most of our clinics in the morning. Tomorrow is Pre-Natal. In the afternoon we have classes—baby care, home nursing, first aid. Public Health covers quite a wide range. In many cities it includes home nursing care and visiting school nurse." She paused long enough to take a swallow of coffee and pour the last quarter cup into the sink. "I'll never learn to make coffee without the telltale dregs in the bottom of the cup. Dr. Tipton says it's genuine battery acid, but good. I think I hear him now. You girls stay and finish yours if you like. I'll get the patients started."

Julia and Lou Ellen served chiefly in the role of observers. The well-oiled machinery of the clinic needed no help

118

in its smooth operation, in the easy flow of patients, the unhurried attention to each question, each examination.

Miss Averill clicked the front door after the final patient and shuddered as the noon whistle, half a block away, began to whine. It gathered force, screeching as its voice, long contained, was suddenly unfettered. A truck lumbered along the street and started the windows vibrating. "The sounds of civilization! For my money, quiet is the best noise!"

Dr. Tipton glanced up from a record page he'd been puzzling over. He smiled at her around the bit of his pipe. "Now, Miss Averill, that all depends on the point of view. If you had half a dozen children, quiet wouldn't be the best noise. It would be a symptom, and a worrying one, at that."

"But, doctor, there are noises and noises. I'm talking about . . . well, at this point I'm not quite sure what I'm talking about. Lunch! That's it. I'm disoriented when I'm hungry. How about you girls? Are you with us for the day? I'll strong-arm Dr. Tipton into a lunch treat, if you are."

Julia grinned. "We'll have to decline the doctor's generous offer. We have a class at one."

"Eyes!" Lou Ellen enlarged. "The anatomy, physiology, and points of refraction thereof. We'll be back in your care and keeping at three, be the good Lord willin' and the creeks don't rise."

Julia tried to hide a triumphant smile as she heard Lou Ellen using Lois' favorite expression. Lou Ellen really belonged, now. Turning to the desk, Julia asked, "Shall we come back here?"

"No." Miss Averill consulted her notebook. "I'm going to make a home call about three. Ordinarily this would be done by the Visiting Nurses but I think you'll enjoy this call. It's near Mercy, too." She jotted down an address, handed it to Lou Ellen. "Suppose you meet me there."

As the stately elm on the corner sundialed three o'clock, Julia followed Lou Ellen up a wide flight of stairs. "I didn't see a Public Health car out in front. Shall we wait at the top of the stairs?"

"She may have been here and gone," Lou Ellen replied. "We'd better ring and ask."

The bell sounded with a deep pleasant bling-blong. The door swung open and Julia gave a happy gasp.

"Why, Jane! Jane Murray!" They met in a fond embrace.

Jane uttered a low guttural sound, stepped back and signaled them in. Warm wood tones reflected patches of the afternoon sunlight. On the bookcase bright amber chrysanthemums nodded in the whisper of air from the doorway. Jane motioned them to a comfortable love seat.

Julia dug in her bag for paper, jotted a note to Jane, and turned to sketch a brief explanation for Lou Ellen. Jane replied to the note with a head shake. Julia said, "Miss Averill hasn't been here yet."

With a cradle motion of her arms, Julia inquired about young Tressa. Jane folded her hands by her cheek.

"Oh, naptime, I see."

The door chime sounded. Jane, glancing at a wall panel where a tiny blue light flashed, excused herself with a nod.

"She talks without saying a word," Lou Ellen marveled.

Miss Averill's voice sounded from the doorway. Julia turned to see fingers flying in conversation. The blue-clad nurse entered, encircled the charming room with a pleased glance, and nodded approval to Jane. Turning to the girls, she said, "I see you have found the Murrays' place. This isn't a usual call. It's for my benefit, not Jane's." She pointed to the wall panel. "See, Joe rigged up a sound receiver system that flashes a red signal when Tressa cries or calls. They had a temporary set-up in the old apartment, but here it's permanent. Jane invited me to see it. She thought it might

120

be helpful to other deaf-mute mothers. Just wait until you see that baby! She's almost a year old and can say a dozen words already."

Julia tucked the hour at the Murray apartment into the special corner of her heart designated for memories of very dear occasions.

The days of Visiting Nurse assignment brought another addition to this memory bank. One January afternoon, the last before reassignment, was unique in that they were given permission to make two calls by themselves. The first, in the North Beach area was to a second-floor flat, dingy on the outside, dreary on the inside.

Julia checked the tarnished brass apartment number against the one on the VNA memo, glanced at Lou Ellen for encouragement, and rapped at the door. A middle-aged woman answered, smiled through a fine mesh of worry lines, and invited them in. Her shoulders drooped heavily, weighted with unused sighs.

"Who's that, Martha?" a voice called from the back of the flat.

"Nurses, Arne. Ones from Mercy. Here to do for you I guess." Made ill at ease by new faces, the woman's fingers wound and unwound a muslin apron, leaving little sunbursts of wrinkles in their wake. "He don't like being found untidy. I'll just straighten his bed some before you go in." She edged away, forcing the droop from her shoulders as she left the room.

Julia took off her coat, clipped on her cap and studied the brief memo again. Charles Arneson, age fifty-seven, chronic myocarditis, routine nursing care.

Lou Ellen shifted uneasily, put the equipment bag down, removed her coat and put it down on the only chair the room boasted. A small table leaned uncertainly against a

121

lumpy day bed. She put on her cap, shoved her hands in the pockets of her apron and paced the floor.

Julia sniffed the air, decided that only homemade vegetable soup could produce such an inviting aroma, and watched the door for Mrs. Arneson's return.

"All right now, girls," the tired voice called and they followed it to the back room. Surprisingly the patient's room was as cheerful and bright as the sidewalk flower stands the girls had passed in downtown San Francisco on the way to this address. Ruffled muslin curtains, a colorful hand-hooked rug, African violets blooming on the window sills, a fine old maple commode serving as a nightstand beside the hospital bed, the room was all that love and hope could make it.

Routine nursing care: a warm bath, soothing backrub, clean linen, oral hygiene, consultation over diet, check of blood pressure, temperature, pulse, respiration, and close observation for signs of toxic reaction to his daily medication. The nursing care took almost an hour and the girls prepared to leave.

"Nurses, you've been so nice." The man spoke in heavy breaths. "Will you let me do something for you?"

Julia explained that they couldn't accept anything but thanked him anyway.

Lou Ellen, ignoring Julia's words, asked, "What is it you want to do, Mr. Arneson?"

The light rekindled in his eyes. "We want to give you. . . . well, our cat has kittens, seven of them. Would you like one? Show them, Martha. Get the box."

"We'd love one. Thank you, Mr. Arneson." Lou Ellen spoke with unusual gentleness.

The cardboard carton bubbled over with its furry assortment. Lou Ellen lifted a tiny ball of toast-colored fur. It unfolded in her hands, spiked a silky tail upward, then recurled in contentment.

As they walked down the steps, Lou Ellen pressed the

kitten toward Julia. "I'll carry the bag and you take care of this. I've never cared much for cats."

A light mist filtering through the cold January afternoon predicted rain so Julia eased the kitten into her raincoat pocket. Her amazement at Lou Ellen's conduct was complete. "If you didn't want it, why did you take it?"

Lou Ellen, answered in a far-away voice. "A long time ago my mother told me, when someone wants to do a kindness, be gracious enough to let him."

"But what are we going to do with it?" Julia asked.

"I don't know. Give it to Ma Marsh, I guess. She's feeding half a dozen cats now. One more won't matter. Where's our next call? A diabetic, isn't it?"

"Yes, a Mrs. Stevens. It's a couple of blocks so we'll have to hurry if we're going to beat the rain."

Lou Ellen walked on in silence.

Julia adjusted a plastic rain bonnet over her hair. "Golly, don't you . . . why Lou Ellen! You're crying. What's wrong?"

Lou Ellen swiped at her cheeks impatiently. "Me! That's what's wrong. I took care of Mr. Arneson a year ago and counted him another moan-and-groaner. He was always talking about his garden and house. They saved for years to buy it, now they've had to sell it. Worse yet, I think they've lost it." A sob, churning in her throat, broke through the words.

"But, he has a wonderful wife. . . . !"

"She is wonderful, isn't she?" Lou Ellen forced her words to a steady tone. "I don't think he even knows how bare the rest of the house is. And the care she's given him certainly shows. All those months in bed and not even a sign of a bedsore! I took care of him for a month and he didn't even remember me." She looked squarely at Julia and said in a matter-of-fact way, "He'd have remembered you."

"Lou Ellen, do you remember telling me once that you

rated a zero on bedside nursing?" Julia asked, voice quiet and sincere. "Now, I think you're one hundred percent. Really I do."

The kitten mewed softly as the girls wiped their shoes on the mat at Mrs. Stevens' door. A clamor sounded within and a voice called out, "Drama, there's someone onna porch. We got company, Drama, we got company."

"Don't just holler, child. See who 'tis."

The door swung open and Molly Franklin's eyes widened until they seemed as big as silver dollars. "Mith Wogers! I knew you'd come. I knew you'd come 'cause you promised."

Julia swallowed a guilty knot in her throat and swooped down to gather the child in a tight hug. "Oh, Molly, God love you! Am I glad to see you!"

A small, gray-haired woman shuffled into the room, wiping her hands on a faded apron. "I take it you're Molly's Miss Rogers. I tried to call you once but you were out. Molly came home right after you left the ward and she was afraid you wouldn't know where to find her. But I see you did. Tch. Tch. Me here talkin' and you girls half froze. Come in. Let me take your coats."

Lou Ellen nodded toward the pair engrossed in each other. "We seem to be unnecessary here, Mrs. Stevens. Shall I check your insulin and diet while they make up for lost time?"

"Mith Wogers, I just waited and waited, but I knew you'd come." Molly beamed.

Julia sat down on the sofa, studied Molly's face for a moment. "You look wonderful, Molly. How are you now and how's your grandmother?"

"Oh, we're fine. I take pills and Drama takes shots and we're gonna go to Los Angeles. My mama wrote in a letter she's gettin' a 'partment. She wants us, Mith Wogers, she wants us alla time. She wrote it in a letter."

Molly snuggled closer and rubbed her fingers over Julia's raincoat draped over the end of the sofa. Suddenly she jerked her hand away, squealing, "Mith Wogers, your coat wiggled!"

Julia gasped. The kitten! Poor thing, it must be smothered. She lifted the pocket flap, felt a lively motion within, and turned to Molly. "Say, little punkin, do you remember about my four hands?"

"I bemember."

Julia scooped up the kitten, brought it out and laid it on Molly's lap. "There you are, Miss Molly. Four hands, all for you!"

Molly giggled. "Mith Wogers, you're funny! Those isn't hands. Those are feets."

17

And Four Forever

Julia thought she might become the first person in medical history whose heart popped, burst, exploded with the wild joy of Spring and San Francisco and love. Through the petal-splattered walks in the park, the green of the Marina, the brilliant orange of the Golden Gate viewed from a sailboat on the bay, Sunday after church brunch high above the ocean at the Cliff House, hot crisp Won Ton in Chinatown, buttered popcorn shared with the pigeons in Union Square, cable car rides to the Wharf for scatter shrimp, her heart brimmed happiness but did not miss a beat. Troy was a splendid guide because he was sharing with her the city he loved. There was time too for get-togethers with his family as well as hers.

Their love grew as true love must grow, one day at a time.

But love and spring and San Francisco were only half of Julia's life—eight hours of each day were spent in Mercy's busy corridors. Because she had completed her classes and her special work she was allowed to choose her assignment. She picked the Emergency Room, sometimes a place of hurried excitement when every skill she'd acquired was needed, and sometimes a place of quiet waiting.

It was during a dull stretch of time one March afternoon that she saw Mrs. Arneson walk past the Emergency Room door. Julia called to her.

The woman turned, looked about. "Did someone call— Oh, hello, Miss. Oh, it's the nurse from . . . Hello, Miss."

Anxiously Julia asked, "Is your husband worse? Is he back in the hospital?"

"Why, no, dear. How nice of you to ask." Her smile had fewer lines to erase than at their last meeting. "I'm here to visit a friend. This is my afternoon out."

"I'm so glad your husband is improving. He must be a lot better to be well enough to leave alone."

"Alone? Oh no, Miss. This is the afternoon Miss Archer comes. Didn't you know? She's been coming once a week ever since you two—you know, the time Arne gave you girls the kitten. My land, I don't know how to tell you what it's meant to us. Arne looks forward to her coming as much as I do." She buttoned her coat up and pulled on gloves. "I must go. Nice to see you, Miss. I'll tell Arne you asked after him."

As the woman pushed through the exit doors, Julia realized the brown coat she wore looked suspiciously like one of Lou Ellen's. Lou Ellen had chosen a unique way to prove herself, but she had learned the secret she sought: how to be the kind of nurse who not only cared *for* her patients, but *about* them, too.

By May first the bulletin board held dozens of announcements of opportunity for the graduating seniors. Scholarships for further study, openings in every field of nursing, in hospitals nearby and half the world away, promises of adventure and challenge.

127

Scattered among the announcements were invitations to a whirl of parties, parties that were only half the fun because Troy was off to Washington, D.C. with the senior partner of the law firm and would not be back until the first of June.

Junior-Senior picnic. Big Basin State Park, May 15, four P.M. Blue jeans and hamburgers. Hikes along the Redwood Trail and wading in the shallow creeks. Potato chips and toasting marshmallows. Crickets chirping, frogs garumping, the crackle of pine surrendering sap to flame in the campfire circle. Steaming coffee, chocolate cake and "gosh, will you ever forget the time. . . ."

Faculty Tea in the living room of the nurses' residence. Sunday afternoon. Silver service gleaming above lacy linen, dainty petit-fours, and midget cups of coffee. Bright conversation among people so long together that silence is comfortable. A surprisingly beautiful Mrs. Braddock in tangerine silk and four-inch heels. "What are your plans after graduation?" Freshmen peeking in from the hallway.

Class night, Thursday, May 20. Songs and skits depicting the foibles and follies of the senior class. Dedication of the annual to Ma Marsh, an easy way to say thank you for being herself. Pens scratching endearments next to photographs of smiles and senior stripes. Dancing to records, thick ham sandwiches and more coffee.

Alumnae Dinner, at the Casa Domingo. Corsages on best dresses, tiny paper replicas of Mercy's cap as place cards, spring broilers and green peas, candlelight and shop talk, "We'd love to have you join the Alumnae. It helps you keep in touch," apple pie and "Private duty is okay but I like office nursing."

Senior Romp, sponsored by the medical staff, at Dr. Deveroux's Skyline estate. Swimming in a heated pool, steaks sizzling over hickory, garlic bread and onion rings. Honkytonk piano and barber shop harmony. Undiluted relaxation.

Graduation Ball, Hotel Saint Francis, June 5.

By seven-fifteen on June 5th the senior floor of the nurses'
home reached the fevered pitch of an amateur fashion show
as twenty-four girls struggled to remove all traces of an on-
duty look. Twenty-four girls sat before twenty-four mirrors
and moaned over twenty-four coiffures that resisted change
from hospital simplicity to hotel elegance. Twenty-four
gowns, some dainty, some daring, promised a kaleidoscope
of color on the ballroom dance floor. The twenty-fifth
gown, ice blue tulle with touches of ice blue satin, hung in
the dismal darkness of a closet and the twenty-fifth girl, in
robe and scuffs, tried not to show her misery.

After all Troy was only doing his duty. Duty was a word
she understood. And he had tried to get home for the dance.
Yesterday's telegram proved how much he wanted to be here
but the negotiations or whatever he was doing in Washington had gone more slowly than expected and might take
another week. The ice blue formal would keep and they
could celebrate her graduation another evening. It was
absolutely silly to be so miserable because of one missed
dance. For that matter she could go to the dance, but why
multiply the misery? Anyone mature enough to be practically a graduate nurse could surmount the disappointment
and spend the evening in a worthwhile way. She could study
for the State Board exams or she could. . . .

"Julia, will you zip me up?" Rosemary, whose date for
the evening was a former patient, turned, inhaled while
Julia zipped the ivory brocade sheath and said, "Do you
think I look too fancy? I mean, he's used to seeing me in
uniform."

"If you want to dress it down a bit, wear your duty oxfords. They'd be comfortable for dancing, too."

Rosemary chuckled. "Don't tempt me, roommate. These
heels are already hurting."

At seven-fifty a dark-eyed freshman stood at the half open

door and said, "Miss Rogers, Ma said to tell you you're fella's here. Golly Miss Rogers, you're not even ready!"

Julia turned from pinning Rosemary's camellia corsage. She doubted the reliability of her ears, the freshman, and the fairy godmother who seemed to be working in her behalf. "Who's here? Troy? He couldn't be. Are you sure? How'd *he* get here? Are you sure it's Troy? Oh, Rosie, go see if it's really Troy. Where's my dress? How will I ever fix my hair? Troy?"

"Easy, Julia. You'll overwork your carburetor racing your motor like that." Rosemary grinned, hurried to the corridor. "Ginny, Lois, Lou Ellen, anybody! Come dress this character while I check to see who awaits in yon parlor."

Five minutes later she returned to the confusion of three girls trying to zip the same zipper. "He's the living, breathing, genuine Troy Archer."

"What a guy!" sputtered Lou Ellen. "He could have called."

"Nope," Rosemary said as she joined the scramble for nylons, hair spray, cologne, and assorted aids to beauty. "The phone's been busy for an hour. Anyway he was lucky to make it. After a last-minute windup of business he went directly to the airport, got a last-minute cancellation, and zoomed west. He didn't even wait for his luggage. He's wearing the judge's dinner jacket and black pants. Hold still, Julia. Here, slide into your left shoe. Where's the other one?"

Lou Ellen checked Julia's hasty hairdo. "That'll never do. Sit down and calm down and I'll fix it for you. If I'd known you were so anxious to go to the dance I'd have arranged a blind date. It must be the dance. Surely you aren't this excited over that brother of mine? Why, I've known him for years and he never affected me this way."

Ma Marsh appeared at the doorway, corsage box in hand.

130

"Mr. Archer's been pacing for fifteen minutes waiting for the florist's delivery. Now that your flowers are here I guess his pacing is for you." She handed Julia the box. "My, don't you girls look nice."

From the waxy green tissue Julia lifted an exquisite white orchid. She pinned it at her waist and raced from the room calling, "Thanks, girls. I'll see you at the dance."

"Julia!" Rosemary moaned. "Come back, Julia. You're wearing only one shoe."

The world turns and hours tick by. Sunrise, sunset, another day is history. But graduation day? Surely, the careful calendar would somehow miss, and graduation would forever be another day away. Her thoughts, her dreams had raced forward to this moment countless times. The custom-tailored, stiff-starched white uniform had hung in her closet for weeks, not to be worn until her student days were accomplished. She had tried it on a dozen times, longing for the right to wear graduate white but not quite believing that the time would come. Now here she was in the beautiful old cathedral, reaching out to accept the alabaster Nightingale lamp with its flaming candle, waiting for the signal to say with her classmates their final pledge to their profession.

In the front row a long line of teachers, supervisors, ward instructors and doctors sat, sharing this final step as they had shared the long, sometimes tedious, always exacting preparation for it. Julia thought back to Mr. Antoine and Molly Franklin, to Mrs. Macadoo and tiny Tressa, to Major Surgery and to first baths, to Rosemary and to Ma, to Lou Ellen and Miss Powell, to days when duty was not so appealing and to times when laughter helped cheat death. Now it was done and she wished it were only beginning. She did not want to trade Mercy Hospital which she knew and loved for the bright, promising future, for that faceless stranger, Tomorrow.

"I solemnly pledge. . . ." Beyond the candle glow, in the darkness of the fifth row Walter Rogers reached for his wife's hand. His gaze remained on the lovely ivory oval of his daughter's face but the warmth of his hand told his divided, therefore multiplied, love.

As the cap came to rest on her shiny blonde hair Julia felt proud and humble. It felt the same as her other caps. For some reason she had expected it to be heavier since it carried a new weight of responsibility. As she stepped back into line, the wide black stripe, mark of respect to the memory of Florence Nightingale, gleamed its velvet beauty under the soft glow of the altar light. Now only the presentation of pins remained before her days at Mercy ended.

Stop, Time! Go back. Julia's glance wandered to the shadows at the side of the church and for one breathless moment she thought time had stalled, whirled backward. A tall, white-haired man walked from the shadows into the light. A bit younger, a bit straighter, he was unmistakably Dr. Carey with the weight of a few years lifted. He placed a large white poster beside the pulpit, eased up the microphone to accommodate his height.

He spoke. "The presentation of the pins will follow. I am Dr. Radford Carey, and I have been asked to make the presentation. As many of you know, a new pin has been designed at the behest and in memory of my late brother, Dr. Clark Carey. It was his wish to see Mercy Hospital represented by a pin which would signify the true meaning of nursing. I am certain that the design selected and executed would meet with his approval." He raised the poster to full view. "May we have the lights, please?"

A click was heard and the nave illuminated. The large

artist's sketch showed a cross formed by the meeting of four hands.

Dr. Carey waited for the stir of interest to subside. "As you can see, the cross bar is formed by the joining of two hands, one symbolizing the compassion of the nurse, the other the skill of the physician. The lower hand, reaching up in hope and trust, is that of the patient. The upper hand, illuminated by shafts of light, reaches down in mercy. It is, of course, the hand of God. The designer of this pin reminds us that God is the Author of Life and the doctor and nurse are its stewards. The vigil over life requires four hands." Dr. Carey lowered the poster.

The rapt attention melted into a low murmur of approval.

"The first pin executed in this design will be awarded to the young woman who conceived the idea. Miss Julia Rogers!"

Julia, as entranced by Dr. Carey's words as those about her, stood without moving. She glanced at the fifth row, saw the elation in her mother's eyes, caught the just perceptible nod of her father's head. Her heart pounding, she moved forward, stood beside Dr. Carey, and accepted the signal honor of the first pin. The tiny clasp secured, Julia ran a caressing finger over the gleaming symbol of Mercy Hospital. A rush of breath carried her thank you to Dr. Carey. For this shining moment Julia felt that another Dr. Carey was present, nodding his approval and smiling at her and all his Mercy girls.

The lamp-lit steps of the cathedral filled quickly as families sought their own. Resigned to the slow progress at the massive arched doorway, Julia stood alone at the side of the wide sweep of the bottom step.

From the darkness behind came a sweetly familiar voice. "Miss Julie Rogers, I thought I'd burst with pride. I sneaked out the side door to find you. Four hands for Mercy . . . what a beautiful idea." As she turned to him, their hands touched, clasped together. "Four hands, Julie—let's join our hands forever."

Before she could answer Julia was swept into a four-way hug by her family. Her smiling eyes said yes to Troy, moved on to Mike, to John, her mother, her father and back to Troy.

Now, the circle of her love complete, Julia was ready to move forward to whatever the future held. Three years before she had said goodbye to her parents but she had not ceased to be a daughter as she became a nurse. So it would be with Mercy. All that was dear to her at Mercy would go with her. Whatever she became—wife, mother, neighbor, friend—in uniform or not—she would always be a nurse.

About the Authors

MARY N. DOLIM was born in Timberhill, Kansas, but grew up in St. Petersburg, Florida. She is a graduate of Mound Park Hospital School of Nursing in St. Petersburg. After her marriage in 1946 she lived in such distant islands as Hawaii and Japan. She now makes her home with her husband, Abel, and two teen-aged children in the San Francisco Bay area of California, the setting for her first girl's book, *Miss Mac,* the story of a young teacher, and for *Four Hands for Mercy.*

Mrs. Dolim became interested in writing in high school and was editor of the school newspaper. "At seventeen," she says, "a career choice seemed so final. I wanted to be a nurse, a teacher, and a writer." She became a nurse, soon learned that a good nurse is also a teacher and finally came to realize that every experience in life is a step toward becoming a writer.

GEN KAKACEK was born in Naperville, Illinois, where she lived until 1953 when she and her husband, Frank, moved to California. Her busy life includes a grown daughter and son, a daughter and son in high school and three young daughters, but she has managed writing time for more than 100 published short stories and articles, two short books for a religious publishing house and an extensive program of lectures in several states. She is a member of the Catholic Press Association.

Both authors studied creative writing under Grace Jones Morgan and Howard Pease and are members of the California Writers' Club. Mrs. Dolim is the author of an adult novel, *The Bishop Pattern,* and is working on another book.

135